Theropods

Confuciusornis

Archaeopteryx

DINOSAURS
+o CHICKENS
How Evolution Works

Gallinuloides
wyomingensis

Chicken

Red jungle fowl

Nick Lund

ILLUSTRATED BY Lucy Rose

WORKMAN PUBLISHING · NEW YORK

Workman Kids
Workman Publishing
Hachette Book Group, Inc.
1290 Avenue of the Americas
New York, NY 10104
workman.com

Workman Kids is an imprint of Workman Publishing, a division of Hachette Book Group, Inc.
The Workman name and logo are registered trademarks of Hachette Book Group, Inc.

Design by Neil Swaab

Cover illustration by Lucy Rose

Workman books may be purchased in bulk for business,
educational, or promotional use. For information, please
contact your local bookseller or the Hachette Book Group
Special Markets Department at special.markets@hbgusa.com.

Library of Congress Cataloging-in-Publication Data is available.

ISBN 978-1-5235-1320-8
ebook ISBNs 978-1-5235-2637-6; 978-1-5235-2638-3; 978-1-5235-2639-0

First Edition August 2024

Printed in China on responsibly sourced paper.

10 9 8 7 6 5 4 3 2 1

CONTENTS

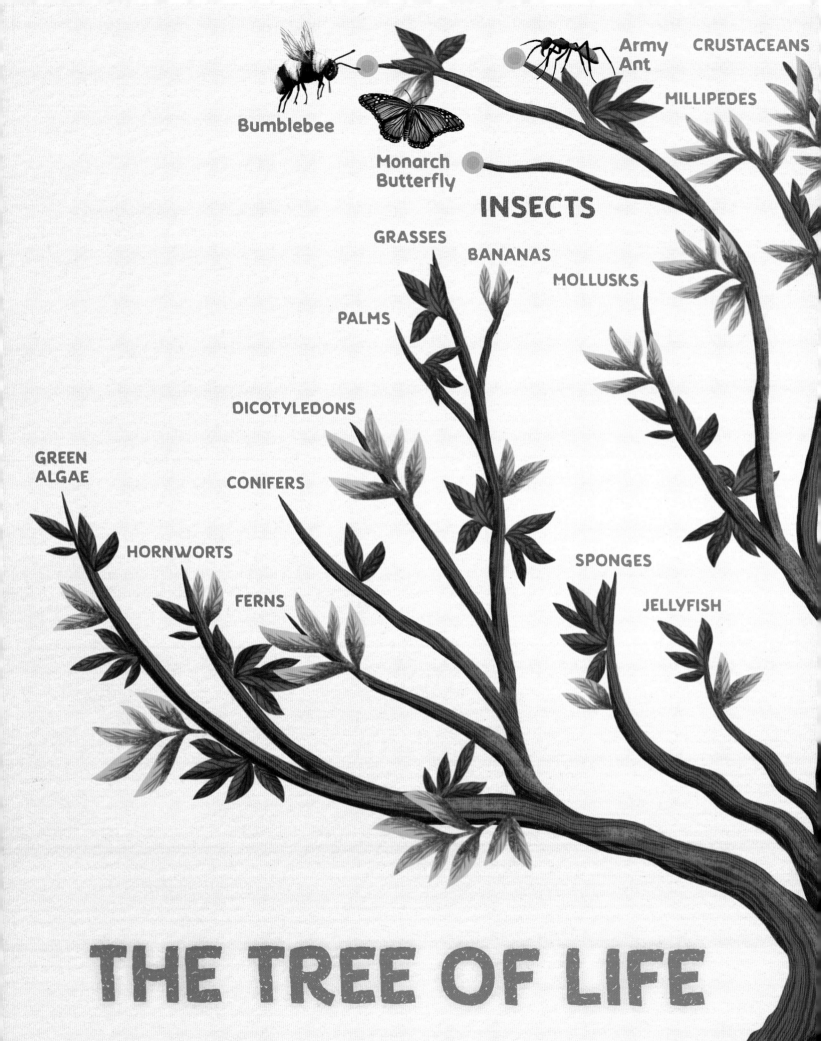

Bumblebee

Monarch
Butterfly

Army
Ant

CRUSTACEANS

MILLIPEDES

INSECTS

GRASSES

BANANAS

MOLLUSKS

PALMS

DICOTYLEDONS

GREEN
ALGAE

CONIFERS

HORNWORTS

SPONGES

JELLYFISH

FERNS

THE TREE OF LIFE

Red Spitting Cobra

Common Box Turtle

Kākāpō

REPTILES

Sword-Billed Hummingbird

American Alligator

BIRDS

Chicken

Giraffe

North American Porcupine

Eastern Gorilla

Mantled Howler Monkey

Human

Horse

Cat

Dog

Blue Whale

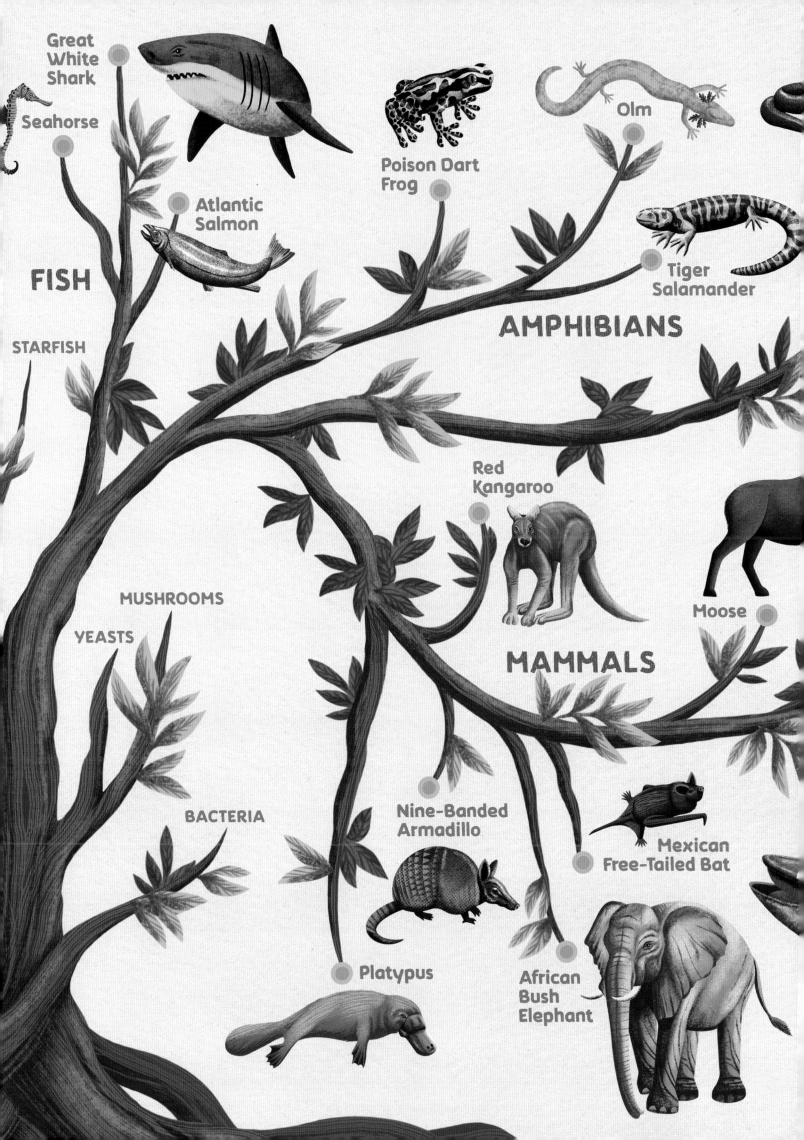

Great
White
Shark

Seahorse

Atlantic
Salmon

FISH

STARFISH

MUSHROOMS

YEASTS

BACTERIA

Poison Dart
Frog

Olm

Tiger
Salamander

AMPHIBIANS

Red
Kangaroo

Moose

MAMMALS

Nine-Banded
Armadillo

Mexican
Free-Tailed Bat

Platypus

African
Bush
Elephant

THE TREE OF LIFE

The Tree of Life is unlike any tree you've ever seen. It's huge, with millions of branches extending in all directions and often tangling together. And it's old: It's been growing for almost four billion years.

Of course, the Tree of Life isn't a *real* tree at all. It's a chart that scientists use to make sense of life on Earth and how it's grown and changed over time. They construct Tree of Life diagrams, also called evolutionary trees or phylogenetic trees, in order to try to understand how different species are related to one another. At the base of the Tree of Life is the earliest known life on the planet, single-celled organisms that emerged more than 3.5 billion years ago. At the tip of each of

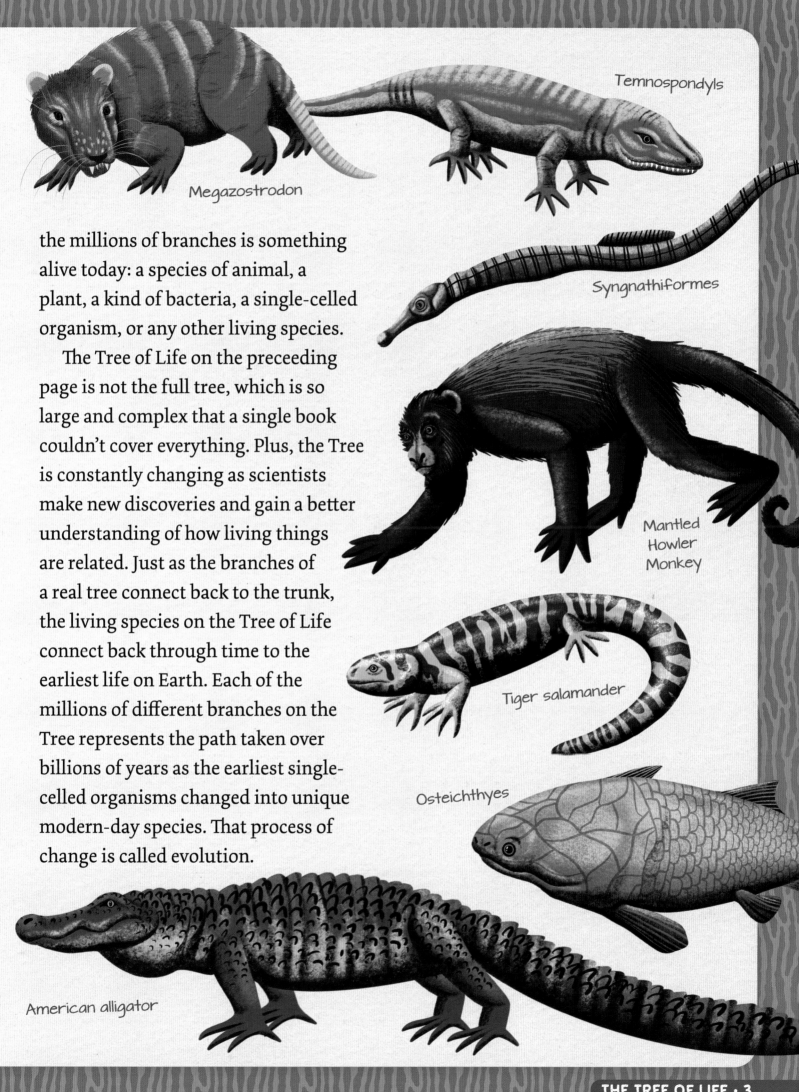

Megazostrodon

Temnospondyls

Syngnathiformes

Mantled
Howler
Monkey

Tiger salamander

Osteichthyes

American alligator

the millions of branches is something alive today: a species of animal, a plant, a kind of bacteria, a single-celled organism, or any other living species.

The Tree of Life on the preceeding page is not the full tree, which is so large and complex that a single book couldn't cover everything. Plus, the Tree is constantly changing as scientists make new discoveries and gain a better understanding of how living things are related. Just as the branches of a real tree connect back to the trunk, the living species on the Tree of Life connect back through time to the earliest life on Earth. Each of the millions of different branches on the Tree represents the path taken over billions of years as the earliest single-celled organisms changed into unique modern-day species. That process of change is called evolution.

EVOLUTION CAUSES THE TREE OF LIFE TO GROW

E volution is the way different kinds of living things have developed over time. Did you know that the ancestors of your cute pet dog were ferocious wolves?

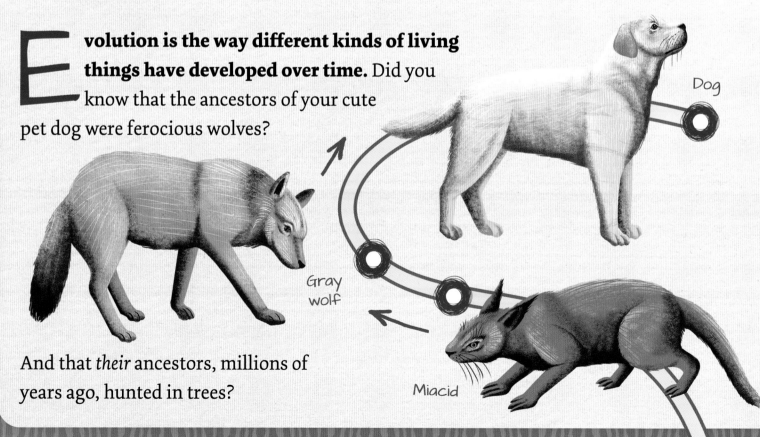

Dog

Gray wolf

Miacid

And that *their* ancestors, millions of years ago, hunted in trees?

And how about the blue whale, the largest creature on Earth—did you know that its ancestors had four legs and lived on land?

Blue whale

Indohyus

Or that ants evolved from wasps? Or that seahorses evolved to hide in sea grass? All the plants and animals and other kinds of life on our planet evolved from a long line of ancestors over millions of years. Their populations slowly changed in response to their environments and the need to survive.

Bumblebee

Evolution seems like a huge concept, but you can see it around you every day. Those beautiful, sweet-smelling flowers in your backyard? They evolved to look and smell like that to attract pollinating insects. Your cat's long, flexible tail? It evolved to be that way to help cats balance. Even you and all other human beings are the products of evolution.

Though you can't necessarily see it happening, all life on Earth is continually evolving. It happens slowly, over the course of many generations, but eventually some of the descendants of one living thing might look different from their ancestors. When that happens, scientists recognize them as a new kind of living thing, and another line is added to the Tree.

This book is about those branches, and what scientists have learned about the paths some of the most fascinating and favorite animals took to get to the tip of the Tree of Life. But we've got a few more items to discuss before we get there, starting with how Earth has been around for a long, long time.

A TIMELINE OF THE

HADEAN EON

4,600 MILLION YEARS AGO

- **Formation of Earth**
  4,500 MILLION YEARS AGO

- **Earth's first oceans form**
  4,400 MILLION YEARS AGO

ARCHEAN EON

4,000 MILLION YEARS AGO

- **First life appears on Earth—simple, single-celled organisms**
  3,850 MILLION YEARS AGO

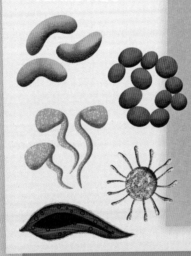

PROTEROZOIC EON

2,500 MILLION YEARS AGO

- **Oxygen begins accumulating in the atmosphere**
  1,500 MILLION YEARS AGO

- **First animals evolve**
  700 MILLION YEARS AGO

- **First invertebrates**
  570 MILLION YEARS AGO

PALEOZOIC ERA

541 MILLION YEARS AGO

- **First fish**
  530 MILLION YEARS AGO

- **First insects**
  480 MILLION YEARS AGO

Scientists have determined that our planet has been around for about 4.5 billion years. The first 600 million years or so were pretty chaotic. There was a lot of matter floating around space in those days, and it all kept smashing into Earth and causing big explosions. It was very hot and very dangerous. But things eventually calmed down and cooled down enough to allow liquid water to form huge oceans. It also became cool enough to allow an atmosphere to form. The first life appeared about a billion years after Earth formed.

HISTORY OF EARTH

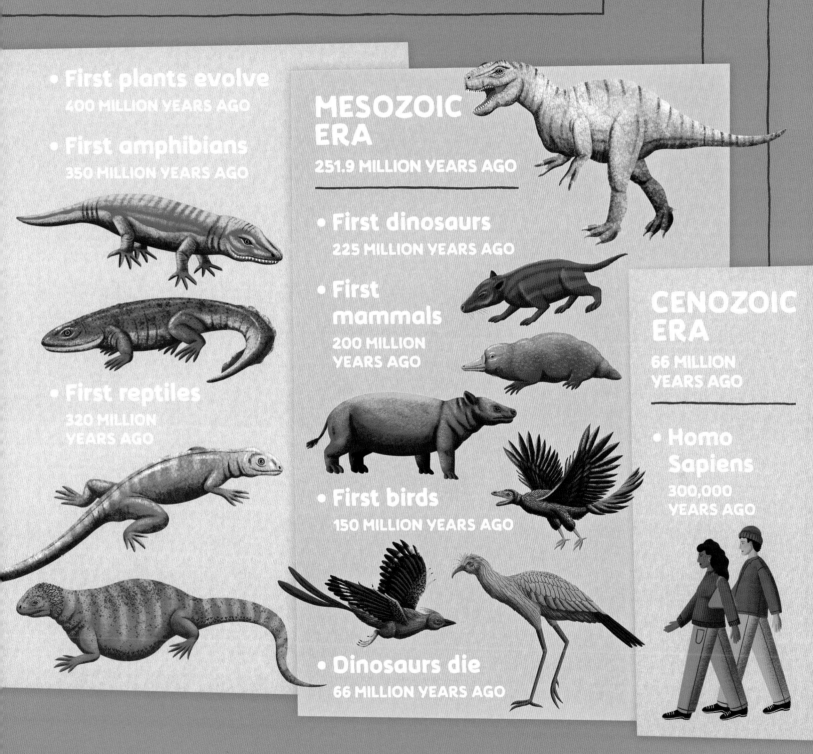

- **First plants evolve**
  400 MILLION YEARS AGO

- **First amphibians**
  350 MILLION YEARS AGO

- **First reptiles**
  320 MILLION YEARS AGO

MESOZOIC ERA
251.9 MILLION YEARS AGO

- **First dinosaurs**
  225 MILLION YEARS AGO

- **First mammals**
  200 MILLION YEARS AGO

- **First birds**
  150 MILLION YEARS AGO

- **Dinosaurs die**
  66 MILLION YEARS AGO

CENOZOIC ERA
66 MILLION YEARS AGO

- **Homo Sapiens**
  300,000 YEARS AGO

The point is that millions of years and billions of years are incredibly long times. And since life on Earth has had 4.5 billion years to evolve, it has gone from tiny cells to become trees, dinosaurs, bacteria, dogs, birds, giant sloths, grass, and every other living thing that is or ever has been. The evolutions shown in this book will be covering hundreds of thousands or millions of years' worth of time. Evolution doesn't have to take that long, but major changes often do.

SO WHAT IS EVOLUTION?

DINOSAURS TO CHICKENS

Evolution is how populations of living things change over time. It's not the way that a single living thing changes over time—how our hair or fingernails grow—but rather changes that occur as one generation gives rise to the next: Parents pass a change on to their children, who may pass it on to their children, who may pass it on to *their* children, and so on. Because evolution occurs across many successive generations, it often can take a very long time for evolutionary changes to show up.

DESCENT WITH MODIFICATION

One concept critical to the idea of evolution is descent with modification. That means, simply, that parents pass on their traits to their children. It works like this: All living things contain special molecules known as DNA (which stands for "deoxyribonucleic acid"). DNA itself is made up of smaller pieces called genes. DNA and its genes are like tiny instruction manuals for life. The DNA inside a bird tells it to grow feathers and a beak, and the DNA inside a tree tells it to grow bark and leaves. Each of us and every other living thing on Earth contains DNA with unique instructions on how we're made.

When organisms reproduce, their offspring inherit the genetic code of their ancestors. That means that genetic code is passed down through new generations for as long as they continue reproducing. In most complex animals, the DNA of one parent combines with the DNA of the other parent to make a new set of DNA for the offspring. The child will grow up to be a unique mix of traits from both parents.

The child may also have some traits that come from the small changes made when the DNA is being copied.

These random and unpredictable changes in DNA are called mutations and may result in the offspring having new traits that may then be passed on to the next generations. Very small changes occurring over generations may result in new living things looking very different from their ancestors.

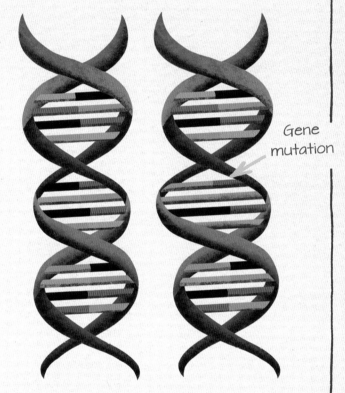

Gene mutation

NATURAL SELECTION

The process of natural selection helps explain which modified traits are passed on to new generations. Life as a wild animal is difficult and dangerous. There may be predators who want to eat you, or you may not be able to find enough food. However, if a creature is born with a mutation that gives it a better chance to survive and reproduce relative to its peers, that creature is more likely to survive and pass that beneficial change on to future generations. This is natural selection.

Some of the new traits may have no impact at all on whether or not an animal survives. For example, a wolf could be born with a mutation that makes one of its claws blue. A blue claw doesn't help that wolf hunt any better, or make it more attractive to mates, but it also doesn't hurt it either. The "blue claw" mutation doesn't affect the wolf in its survival or reproduction.

On the other hand, if a mutation helps an animal survive relative to its peers, it has a better chance of being passed on because an animal that survives may have babies. Examples of beneficial mutations include those that make an animal better at hiding or eluding predators, those that help it find food, or those that make it more attractive to a mate and therefore more likely to reproduce.

At the same time, traits may be lost over time if they no longer give an advantage. For example, certain species of birds lost the ability to fly when they arrived on the islands of New Zealand, which had no native mammals that the birds needed to fly away from (see Kākāpō, page 54).

Living things can only pass on their DNA if they survive to reproduce, and so any changes that help a creature survive are more likely to be passed on.

WHAT DRIVES EVOLUTION?

Animals evolve in all kinds of ways and for many different reasons. Here are some factors that drive change:

SAFETY

Animals need to stay alive in order to reproduce, so they evolve all kinds of traits to protect themselves from predators. Porcupines' mammalian hair evolved into sharp spines.

Mice stay hidden during the day and come out only at night, when there are fewer predators around. They evolved whiskers to help them move around in the dark. Deer and antelope evolved speed to help them outrun their attackers. Many creatures have evolved camouflage coloration, helping them blend in with their surroundings and making it more difficult for predators to see them. These adaptations can literally mean the difference between life and death for animals.

FOOD

Species evolve in all kinds of ways to help keep themselves fed. Many predator species have evolved some of the same traits used by their prey, like camouflage and speed, to give themselves a better chance at catching their next meals. Giraffes evolved long necks to help them reach leaves that no other animals were eating. Finches evolved strong bills to

help them crack open seeds. There are far too many examples to name here, but offspring born with inherited features that help them stay fed are more likely to pass those features on to future generations.

ATTRACTING A MATE

Animals have evolved in all kinds of interesting ways to better their chances at impressing potential partners. If an animal can't attract a mate, it's not going to pass its genes along. Many animals, like deer and sheep, have evolved horns or antlers to help males fight one another, with the female choosing the strongest. Some species of birds have developed elaborate plumages and showy dances to prove their worthiness.

Oddly, the process of animals adapting features to impress potential mates, called sexual selection, can run in opposition to developing features that help in natural selection. Big antlers make it harder for deer to walk through the forest. Bright feathers make birds more visible to predators.

However, if features like bright feathers or big antlers increase the chance that a bird or deer will pass on its genes, those traits are likely to persist because they may keep the species alive.

ISOLATION

Animals living on islands often have different experiences than those on the mainland. There may be less food on islands, but there also may be fewer predators. The unusual pressures of island life often drive species to take new forms. Sometimes a lack of food causes species to become smaller than their mainland relatives, such as with certain species of dwarf chameleons on islands off Madagascar, or the small subspecies of white-tailed deer living on the Florida Keys. Other species may get bigger on islands, typically when there are fewer predators around. Many New Zealand bird species are examples of this phenomenon, and so is the dodo, a giant pigeon that used to live on the island of Mauritius. These "islands" don't need to be oceanic islands but rather any area cut off from its surroundings, including freshwater lakes cut off from the ocean, mountaintops, and forests split by grasslands or rivers.

OPPORTUNITY

An overarching factor driving evolutionary change is opportunity. Where there are ecological niches waiting to be filled, animals can evolve to fill them. Ecological niches are the specific roles that species can play in an environment, such as flying around at night catching insects (bat) or drinking the nectar out of deep flowers (hummingbird). When niches become available, whether through an extinction, a change in the landscape, or otherwise, new species have an opportunity to fill them. The best example of this may be the process known as "adaptive radiation," which is when a whole bunch of new species evolve fairly quickly from a single species or group. The most famous example is the radiation of mammals after the extinction event that ended the age of the dinosaurs. Mammals were

mostly small, nocturnal mouselike creatures when the dinosaurs were around. But the ones that survived the asteroid impact quickly radiated to fill many of the ecological niches the dinosaurs left, including those of large predators (lions and bears), sea giants (whales), and heavy herbivores (elephants and hippopotamuses). These bursts of rapid evolutionary change are common for all kinds of species—when they get the opportunity to grow.

EVOLUTION IS NOT A MARCH TOWARD PERFECTION

While there is a general trend over the millions of years in which animals have existed for them to grow more complex, evolution isn't driving toward any particular goal or end point. A species that has evolved to be a fit for its environment may find itself quickly extinct when that environment changes. Earlier animals weren't any less successful than modern creatures; they just didn't adapt to an ever-changing world.

WHAT IS A SPECIES?

Golden eagle

Bald eagle

A species is a group of animals that look different from other groups of animals. Blue whales are a species of whale. Red-crowned parrots are a species of parrot.

The term "species" is more useful to distinguish animals that are closely related. Bald eagles are a species of eagle. Golden eagles are a different species of eagle. They're both eagles, and they're similar in many ways, but they're different enough from each other that they're different species. Bald eagles have different-colored feathers than golden eagles, and they eat different things and live in different habitats. There are many ways in which species can be different from one another.

It seems simple enough, but the idea of "species" is messy in practice. In fact, scientists can't agree on a single definition for what a "species" is, or necessarily for which groups of animals are part of a single species and which are part of multiple species. One possible definition for "species" is "the largest group of individuals possible where all those in the group can reproduce and make fertile offspring with one another." So, by that definition, an African bush elephant and an American alligator are not the same species because they can't make babies together.

Seems straightforward enough. However, it's not uncommon for different species, especially ones that are closely related, to produce fertile young together. These offspring are called hybrids. Some hybrids you might know are mules, the offspring of horses and donkeys, and "coywolves," the offspring of coyotes and wolves. Scientists are continually refining their understanding of the species concept and examining the squishy boundaries between what we think of as different species.

HOW TO USE THIS BOOK

Presented in the following pages are some examples of how species *may* have evolved over millions of years to reach their modern-day forms. By "may," I mean that scientists are using the incomplete information they've learned from the study of fossils and DNA to try to piece together the story of evolution. Some scientists disagree with one another, and new discoveries that change our understanding of the evolutionary pathways of certain animals are being made all the time. Those are all part of the scientific process.

Each chart focuses on a modern species and traces its evolutionary pathway back through time. The animals in each chart do not necessarily form a chain of direct ancestry from one to another. Instead, the charts feature creatures—and their relevant traits— that are some of the closest relatives that scientists have discovered so far or are part of closely related lineages.

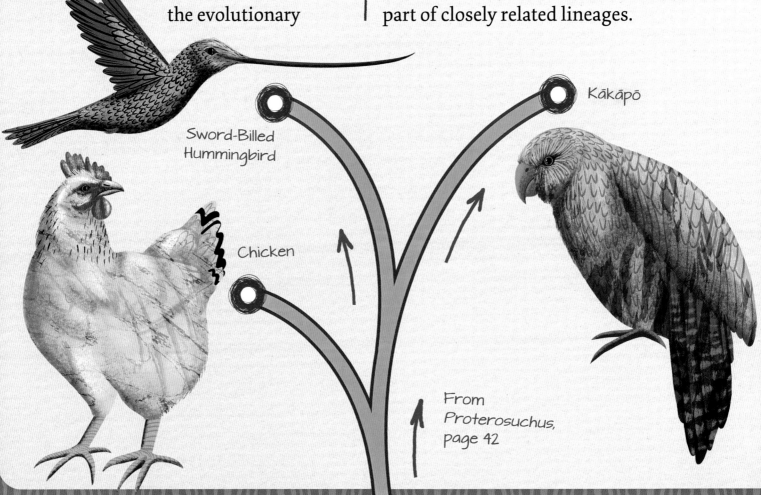

Sword-Billed Hummingbird

Kākāpō

Chicken

From Proterosuchus, page 42

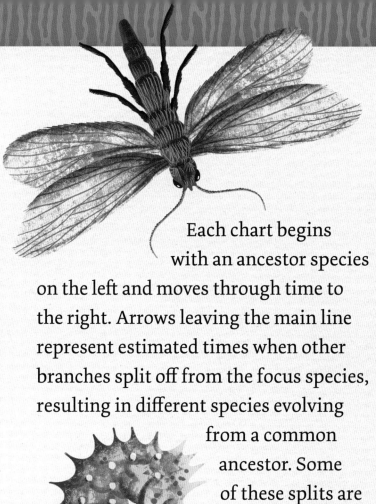

Each chart begins with an ancestor species on the left and moves through time to the right. Arrows leaving the main line represent estimated times when other branches split off from the focus species, resulting in different species evolving from a common ancestor. Some of these splits are illustrated in other pages, while others are there just to give you a sense of how certain animals are related to one another. There are many, many splits that aren't represented at all because there simply isn't room in this book to show them all!

The species in this book were chosen because they represent some of the major groups of animals: insects, fish, amphibians, reptiles, birds, and mammals. These are just a tiny fraction of the animals on Earth, and animals are themselves just a tiny fraction of all life on Earth, which also includes bacteria, single-celled organisms, plants, fungi, algae, and others. The charts in this book are a simplification of extremely complex and uncertain science and are meant to give you an understanding of how evolution works and how new species develop, grow, and either survive or die off.

Most of the animals presented are ones that have been found as fossils. Scientists have a number of ways to get a pretty good idea of the age of different fossils, but fossils are hard to find. Scientists know that what we've found as fossils represents just a tiny fraction of all the creatures that have lived on Earth.

Some animals presented in this book have never actually been found, but scientists have assumed their existence and placement on the timeline through studying a species' "molecular clock." Scientists believe that by comparing certain DNA sequences, they can get a general sense of how long ago two branches split away from a common ancestor. This means they can estimate the time a common ancestor lived, even if they've never found its fossils. Science is just that awesome.

What comes next is a story about the history of life and its changes. It's not a promise to you that we know anything with complete certainty. So your job as the reader is to ask questions, do more research, and think for yourself. There's been a lot of evolution on this planet, and you, reader, are as advanced as it gets. Let's see what other connections we can make.

HOW ARE THINGS ORGANIZED?

DOMAIN
Eukarya

KINGDOM
Animalia

PHYLUM
Chordata

CLASS
Aves

ORDER
Accipitriformes

FAMILY
Accipitridae

GENUS
Haliaeetus

SPECIES
Haliaeetus leucocephalus

There are lots and lots of living things, and scientists need a way to keep track of them all. So scientists organize the relationships living things have to one another with a system called taxonomy. It's set up like a big upside-down pyramid, with the category at the top containing a lot of different related living things and the category at the bottom containing just one group of very closely related living things. There are eight main levels, or ranks: domain, kingdom, phylum, class, order, family, genus, and species.

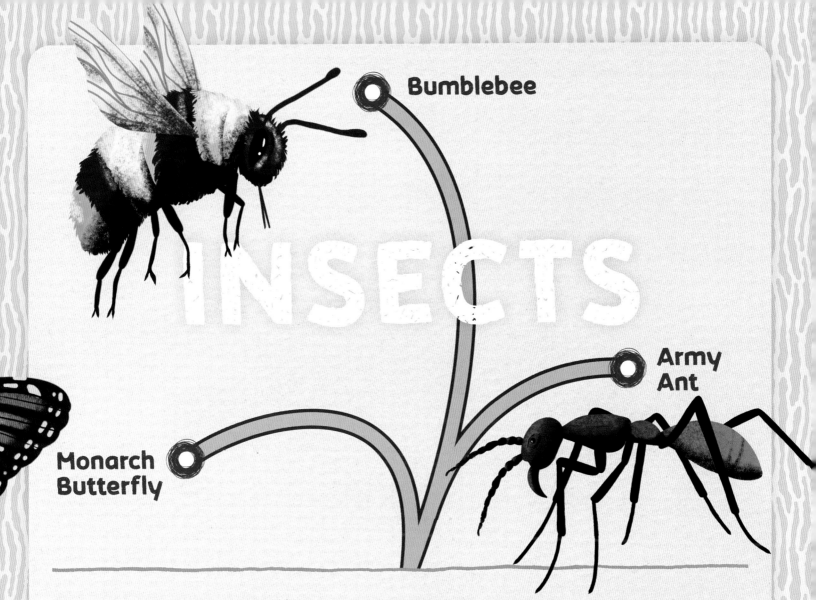

INSECTS

Bumblebee

Army Ant

Monarch Butterfly

No group of creatures is as diverse as the insects. Scientists have found more than a million different species of insects currently living on Earth, and they're finding new ones all the time. In their hundreds of millions of years on Earth, insects have evolved ways to live almost everywhere: underground, in the treetops, and in the air. Though they're small, their diversity and adaptability make insects the most successful group of animals on the planet.

The ancestors of insects lived under the sea. They are believed to have been arthropods, animals with segmented bodies protected by hard exoskeletons. At some point, maybe as long as 500 million years ago, scientists believe that a type of arthropod called a crustacean crawled out of the water. While the crustaceans that remained in the water would eventually become modern-day crabs and lobsters, the crustaceans that made their way onto dry land would eventually become insects and proceed to crawl, dig, and fly all over Earth.

Three familiar insects—the monarch butterfly, the army ant, and the bumblebee—illustrate just a few of the many different forms insects have evolved into over their history.

MONARCH BUTTERFLY

The beautiful monarch butterfly is one of the most famous insects on Earth. Monarchs are known for their incredible migrations. Each fall, monarchs flee the dropping temperatures in the northern fields and backyards in the United States and Canada and fly thousands of miles to the warmth and safety of pine forests in Mexico, and then they return again in the spring.

Modern-day monarchs have come a long way from their earliest insect ancestors, which first appeared back in the Devonian period more than 400 million years ago.

Insect Beginnings

Rhyniella (≈400 mya)

Fossils of the earliest insects are very difficult to find and interpret, but the tiny fossilized remains of a creature named *Rhyniella praecursor* give scientists some insight into the origins of insects.

To the army ant, page 22

To grasshoppers, earwigs, mantises, cockroaches, beetles, and other insects

Taking to the Air

Agathiphaga (≈250 mya)

Agathiphaga were some of the earliest moths, and they made use of an incredibly helpful adaptation that had appeared first among the insects: wings. The ability to fly helped insects find food, escape predators, and lay eggs in places that predators couldn't reach. Two species of *Agathiphaga* still exist today in Australia and remote Pacific islands, living only in rare, ancient kauri trees.

Big Wings

With a wingspan of up to a foot, the Queen Alexandra's birdwing from the island of Papua New Guinea holds the crown as the world's largest butterfly.

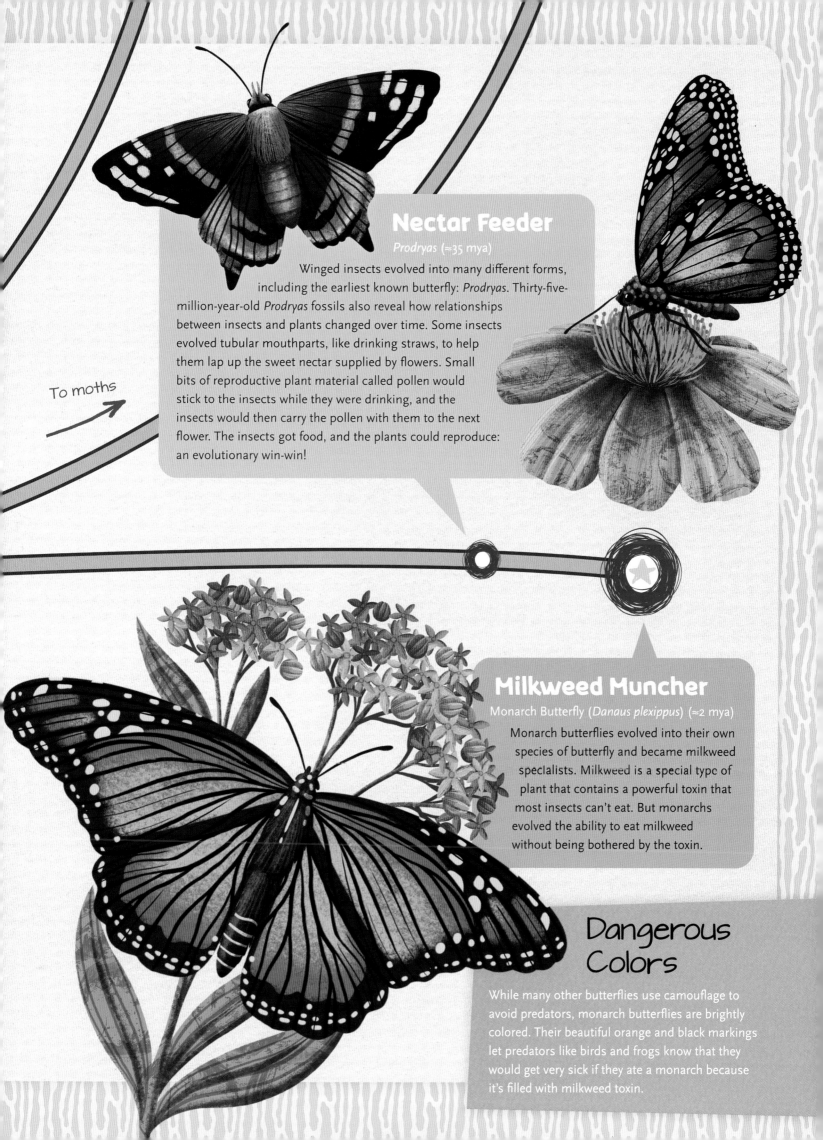

Nectar Feeder

Prodryas (≈35 mya)

Winged insects evolved into many different forms, including the earliest known butterfly: *Prodryas*. Thirty-five-million-year-old *Prodryas* fossils also reveal how relationships between insects and plants changed over time. Some insects evolved tubular mouthparts, like drinking straws, to help them lap up the sweet nectar supplied by flowers. Small bits of reproductive plant material called pollen would stick to the insects while they were drinking, and the insects would then carry the pollen with them to the next flower. The insects got food, and the plants could reproduce: an evolutionary win-win!

To moths

Milkweed Muncher

Monarch Butterfly (*Danaus plexippus*) (≈2 mya)

Monarch butterflies evolved into their own species of butterfly and became milkweed specialists. Milkweed is a special type of plant that contains a powerful toxin that most insects can't eat. But monarchs evolved the ability to eat milkweed without being bothered by the toxin.

Dangerous Colors

While many other butterflies use camouflage to avoid predators, monarch butterflies are brightly colored. Their beautiful orange and black markings let predators like birds and frogs know that they would get very sick if they ate a monarch because it's filled with milkweed toxin.

ARMY ANT

Ants are considered some of the most successful animals in history despite their size. They live everywhere except Antarctica and are estimated to have a population of 10 million billion individuals. But ants looked very different early in their evolutionary history. Their ancestors in the Triassic evolved a special tool to lay eggs, which eventually formed into a deadly weapon: a wasp's stinger. Some of these flying wasps became ground dwellers and eventually diversified into the more than 10,000 species of ants alive today.

Advanced Egg Layer
Xyelidae (≈200 mya)

Early insects laid their eggs on the ground, where they were at risk from predators and weather. But a group of sawflies called Xyelidae had a special tool on their backsides—a needlelike organ called an ovipositor—that helped them and other early relatives to lay eggs directly into plants or down deeper into the ground, where they had a better chance of survival.

A New Weapon
Aculeata (≈170 mya)

Certain insects would discover that having needles on their bodies was good for more than just laying eggs. Emerging sometime in the middle of the Jurassic, Aculeata wasps used their sharp ovipositors for defense—and the stinger was born. Wasps now had a powerful tool to subdue smaller prey like caterpillars for food, and also to defend themselves and their colonies from larger insect predators.

From Rhyniella, page 20

Ouch!

Because stingers evolved from the egg-laying organs of female insects, only female bees and wasps have them.

Armies of Army Ants

The term "army ant" is used to refer to many different kinds of ants on different continents that use the same rampaging hunting style, though scientists believe that all these ants evolved from a single unknown ancestor.

Out of the Skies and Underground

Ant-Like Wasp (≈150 mya)

Stingers proved to be a great advantage and helped wasps radiate into thousands of different species in different ecological niches. Some wasps came out of the air and spent their time looking for food on the ground. Some of these ground wasps eventually lost their wings entirely. However, ants retained their stingers and didn't give up flying completely. Though not a direct ancestor of modern ants, and believed to have lived after other ants had already evolved, *Sphecomyrma* is one of the oldest fossil ants ever found and illustrates combined traits of ants and stinging wasps.

An Army of Ants

Eciton burchellii (≈100 mya)

Ants diversified into thousands of different species. Most species live in large colonies where the responsibilities to find food, raise young, defend the nest, and other duties are split into highly organized divisions. Army ants organize to form massive hunting raids. In the jungles of Central and South America, one species of army ant, *Eciton burchellii*, sends a river of up to 200,000 individual ants across the forest floor to capture and dismember any small creatures unlucky enough to be in the way!

To the bumblebee, page 24

To carpenter ants, bullet ants, fire ants, and other ant species

BUMBLEBEE

Watching bumblebees buzz from flower to flower collecting pollen is one of the joys of summer, but the ancestors of bees weren't so friendly. After the ovipositors of earlier insects evolved into stingers (see Army Ant, page 22), many wasps used their new weapons to catch other insects. But eventually, some wasps evolved a taste for pollen instead of prey, and the bees were born. Today, more than 20,000 different species of bees exist on Earth, and they play a critical role in pollinating plants and producing honey.

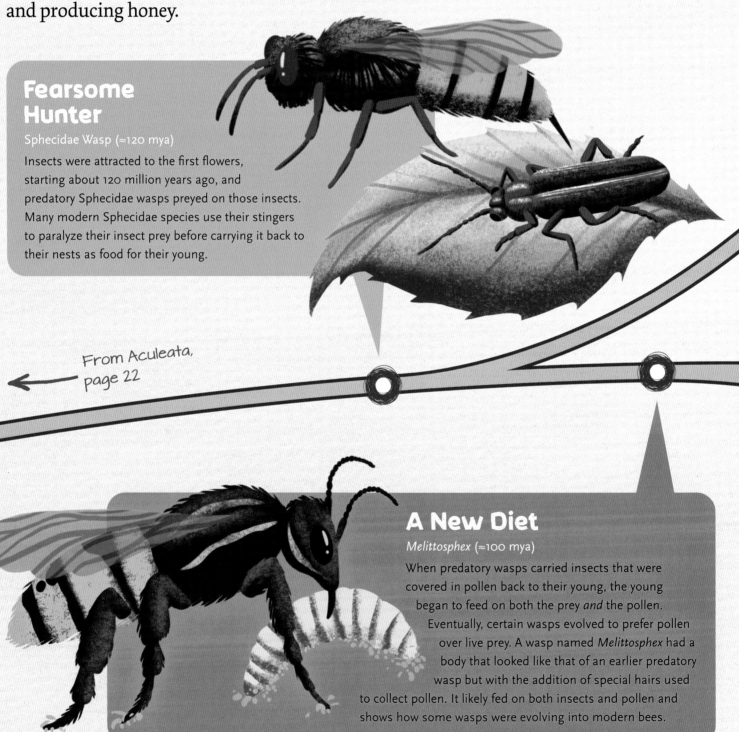

Fearsome Hunter
Sphecidae Wasp (≈120 mya)

Insects were attracted to the first flowers, starting about 120 million years ago, and predatory Sphecidae wasps preyed on those insects. Many modern Sphecidae species use their stingers to paralyze their insect prey before carrying it back to their nests as food for their young.

From Aculeata, page 22

A New Diet
Melittosphex (≈100 mya)

When predatory wasps carried insects that were covered in pollen back to their young, the young began to feed on both the prey *and* the pollen. Eventually, certain wasps evolved to prefer pollen over live prey. A wasp named *Melittosphex* had a body that looked like that of an earlier predatory wasp but with the addition of special hairs used to collect pollen. It likely fed on both insects and pollen and shows how some wasps were evolving into modern bees.

To wasps
and hornets

To Bee or Not to Bee?

The distinctive shape and coloration of bees lets predators know that these insects pack a powerful sting and should be left alone. Because it's safe to look like a bee, many harmless insects have become bee mimics. Certain species of hoverflies, bee flies, and even beetles have evolved similar colors, patterns, and body shapes to trick predators.

Backyard Buddy

Bumblebee (≈40 mya)

Once bees turned to collecting pollen, natural selection favored those that could carry more of it. Some bees found that pollen could stick to the hairs on their legs and eventually evolved special "pollen baskets"— cavities surrounded by hairs that could trap pollen and store it while the bees were flying. Some of these pollen-collecting Apinae bees became bumblebees. They have large, round bodies covered in fuzzy hairs and bright colors to warn off predators. These large bees can carry up to 75 percent of their body weight (which is still less than one gram) in pollen!

Biggest Bumble

The largest bumblebee species in the world is Bombus dahlbomii, a nearly two-inch-long bee from southern Chile and Argentina that has been called by ecologist Dave Goulson "a monstrous, fluffy ginger beast."

To honeybees and
orchid bees

How Scientists Reconstruct the Past

Scientists called paleontologists work to find and understand ancient forms of life. They often work with fossils, which are the preserved remains of once-living things.

A fossil is usually made when an organism is covered in sediment, like sand or lava, soon after its death. Minerals from the sediment eventually permeate the dead creature and it becomes a fossil.

Fossils are tough to find. Most living things that die decompose, and so their bodies are only preserved if they're quickly covered in sediment, trapped in amber, or preserved in other ways. The vast majority of dead things did not become fossils, so paleontologists have to be smart—and lucky—to find those that did. We've found only a tiny fraction of the life that used to exist on this planet, and scientists don't know what else might be out there.

Once a paleontologist finds a fossil, they must carefully excavate it from the ground, then try to understand what it looked like as a living creature. They can use clues from the rock layers to estimate how long ago it lived. Still, there is a lot that we'll never know for sure, and new discoveries are being made all the time.

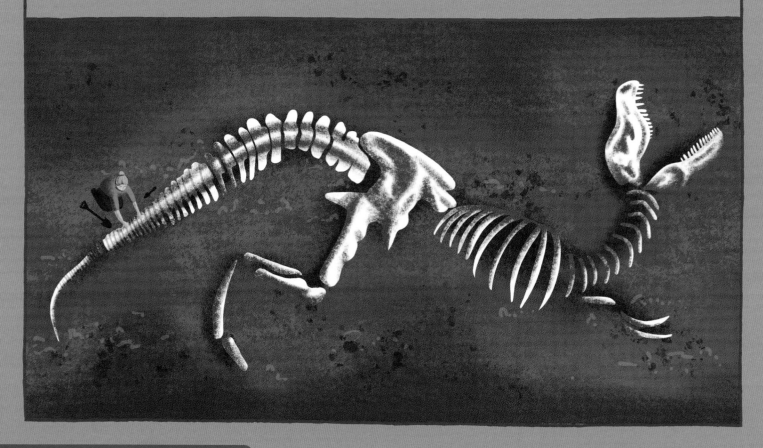

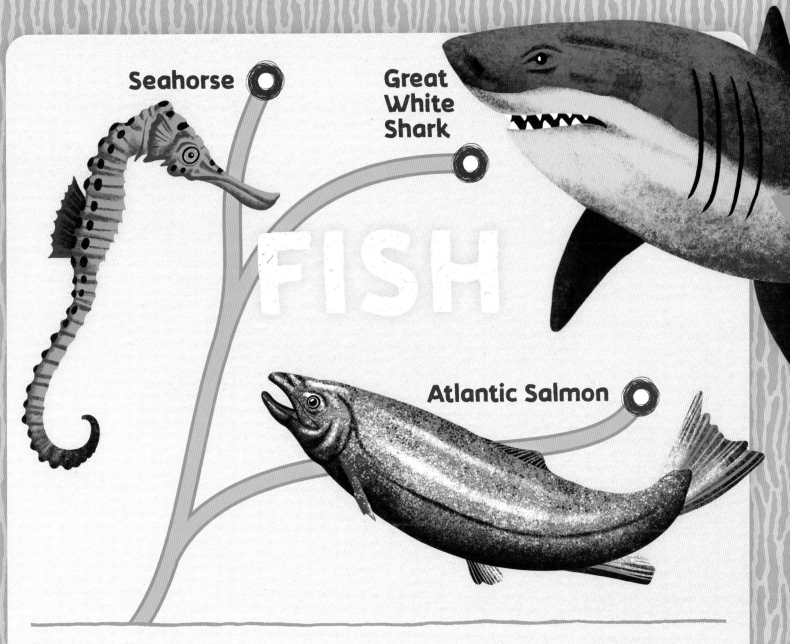

Seahorse

Great White Shark

FISH

Atlantic Salmon

Five hundred million years ago, the seas were dominated by creatures called arthropods. But other creatures were emerging, ones with cords of nerves running through their soft bodies. These nerves eventually evolved into bones that protected vital organs while allowing for greater range of movement and the ability to grow much larger.

Fish are the oldest and most diverse vertebrates, having spread to nearly every aquatic habitat, both freshwater and saltwater, on Earth. There are nearly 35,000 known species of fish on our planet, with many more likely still to be discovered. They've evolved to take many shapes and sizes—from tiny colorful reef fish to massive tuna—and live in every possible underwater habitat, including in the complete darkness at the very bottom of the sea.

Out of those thousands of fish species, there are three that help explain how evolution split the fish into many different shapes and lifestyles: the Atlantic salmon, the seahorse, and the great white shark.

ATLANTIC SALMON

Salmon are some of the most well-known fish in the world, featured in the mythologies of cultures around the globe and appearing on millions of dinner plates every night. Most salmon species are anadromous, meaning they spend their adult lives in salt water but travel up into freshwater rivers and streams to lay eggs. This amazing behavior is the result of hundreds of millions of years of evolution, which saw fish grow from tiny creatures with nature's first backbones to a massively diverse group of animals living in almost every body of water on Earth.

Go Fish

Haikouichthys (≈525 mya)

The first fish looked similar to the small minnows that are around today. *Haikouichthys* had a large fin that ran down its back and around to its underside to help propel it forward in the water, and gills on the sides of its body to help extract oxygen from the water.

Jaw Awe

Placoderm (≈430 mya)

Fish grew larger over the next hundred million years, and they took on new shapes. Placoderms evolved bony armor to protect them from predatory arthropods. They also had jaws, which allowed their mouths to open and close, and helped them catch and hold slippery prey. Jaws also allowed them to breathe more efficiently by helping pump water over their gills.

To hagfish and lampreys

Homeward Bound

Atlantic salmon return to fresh water each year to lay their eggs, and each fish returns to the exact same stretch of the exact same river! Scientists believe they use Earth's magnetic field to help them find their home river and then use their sense of smell to sniff out their home section.

Boning Up

Osteichthyes (≈420 mya)

As fish continued to evolve, they split into two different groups: those with bodies made of an elastic tissue called cartilage and those with skeletons made of bones. The bony fish were called Osteichthyes. The earliest bony Osteichthyes had simple lungs in addition to gills to help them breathe.

Flex to Success
Actinopterygii (≈300 mya)

Millions of years later, another branch of the fish line broke off from Osteichthyes and conquered the world. Actinopterygii had specialized jaw bones that could extend out of the body to more effectively snatch prey out of the water. They also had more flexible fins and tails, allowing them to be faster and more maneuverable swimmers. These adaptations and others allowed Actinopterygii to flourish into many different forms. Today, about 96 percent of all living fish are Actinopterygii, and they've diverged into more than 26,000 different species.

Long Shot

Despite being born in the relative safety of freshwater streams, young Atlantic salmon still face many dangers. Of the up to 10,000 eggs laid by a female Atlantic salmon, fewer than 10 will survive to become adults, mainly due to predators like larger fish, seabirds, and marine mammals hoping to snatch up a young salmon.

To lobe-finned fishes, amphibians, reptiles, birds, and mammals

To the seahorse, page 30, and catfish, piranhas, eels, clown fish, and many other fish

Swimming Upstream
Salmonid (≈100 mya)

Among the many groups of fish to evolve from the Actinopterygii was a group of long-bodied strong swimmers called salmonids, which today includes fish like trout, whitefish, char, and salmon. Some salmonids are famous for being born in fresh water, but they spend most of their lives in the ocean. Salmonids travel far up freshwater rivers and streams to lay their eggs in areas where there are fewer predators. After growing up in the relative safety of the rivers, the young fish eventually migrate to the ocean, where there is more food and more room to swim.

To the great white shark, Page 32

Atlantic Action
Atlantic Salmon (≈10,000 years ago)

One type of salmonid began migrating up new rivers in the North Atlantic ocean that were exposed at the end of the last ice age. These fish became a species now known as the Atlantic salmon, and they can still be found migrating up rivers in the United States, Canada, Norway, Russia, and other North Atlantic countries.

To trout, whitefish, and char

SEAHORSE

Seahorses may look more like dragons or underwater fairies, but they're actually fish shaped by millions of years of evolution. At least 46 seahorse species are known to exist, found mostly in warm oceans. Their ancestors lived in beds of sea grass and evolved long, thin, flexible bodies to stay camouflaged and hunt for small crustacean prey.

To bass, sunfish, marlins, angelfish, and many more

A New School of Fish
Perciformes (≈100 mya)

Perciformes, a large and diverse group of modern fish with spiny fins, developed out of the Actinopterygii line (see page 29). These fins are thought to have given them even more flexibility underwater, making it easier for them to catch prey and elude predators.

From the Actinopterygii, page 29

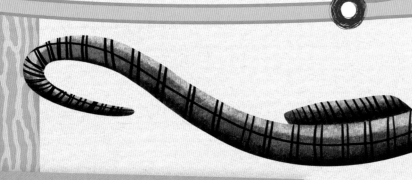

Role Reversal

Unusually and somewhat mysteriously, seahorses also evolved a different reproductive strategy than other fish. Female seahorses deposit fertilized eggs into special pouches in the males' bodies. The males then eventually give birth to baby seahorses. Scientists are not totally sure why seahorses made this switch, but it may be to allow the females to develop new eggs more quickly.

Sneaky and Stealthy
Syngnathiformes (≈50 mya)

Perciformes evolved into many different body shapes, and one of them was meant for camouflage. Long, thin bodies helped the Syngnathiformes blend in with beds of sea grass, where they could hide from predators and also surprise small shrimp and other crustaceans that got too close.

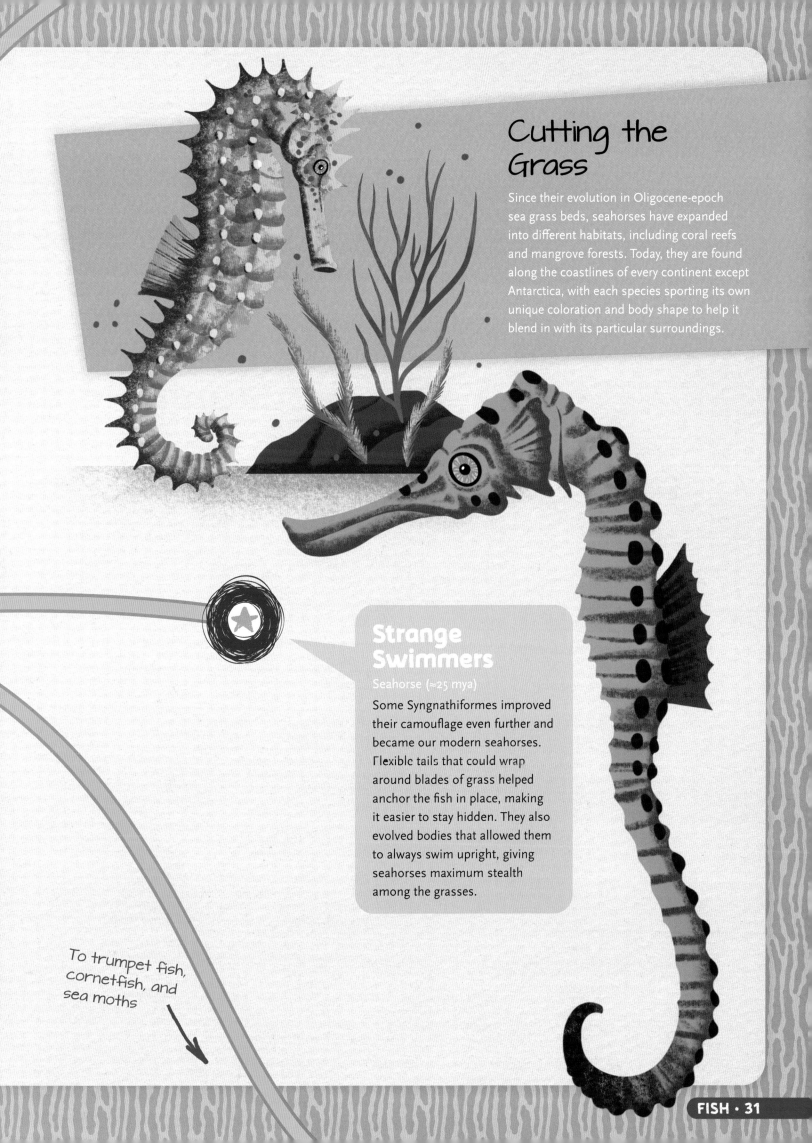

Cutting the Grass

Since their evolution in Oligocene-epoch sea grass beds, seahorses have expanded into different habitats, including coral reefs and mangrove forests. Today, they are found along the coastlines of every continent except Antarctica, with each species sporting its own unique coloration and body shape to help it blend in with its particular surroundings.

Strange Swimmers

Seahorse (≈25 mya)

Some Syngnathiformes improved their camouflage even further and became our modern seahorses. Flexible tails that could wrap around blades of grass helped anchor the fish in place, making it easier to stay hidden. They also evolved bodies that allowed them to always swim upright, giving seahorses maximum stealth among the grasses.

To trumpet fish, cornetfish, and sea moths

GREAT WHITE SHARK

Sharks have been among the ocean's fiercest predators for hundreds of millions of years. Early on, they evolved the body of an effective swimming predator—torpedo-shaped, streamlined, with lots of sharp teeth— and it's helped them survive through several major extinction events and all the other changes Earth has endured. Sharks remain the fiercest predators in the oceans, with none more feared than the great white shark.

Call a Dentist!

Much of what we know about shark evolution comes from scientists analyzing shark teeth. Cartilage doesn't fossilize very well, but teeth do. The fossilized teeth of ancient sharks can still be easily found on beaches in Florida, the Carolinas, and elsewhere in the Southeast.

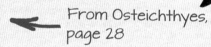
← From Osteichthyes, page 28

Devonian Devils

Cladoselache (≈380 mya)

While some fish grew bony skeletons, another line of fish evolved skeletons made out of an elastic tissue called cartilage. Ditching heavy bones made these fish lighter and faster, which was a big advantage for hunting. A group called *Cladoselache* became even more agile after evolving a streamlined body and deeply forked tail. These marine predators were some of the first sharks.

The Age of Oddities

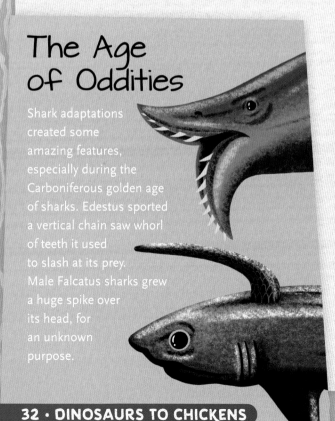

Shark adaptations created some amazing features, especially during the Carboniferous golden age of sharks. Edestus sported a vertical chain saw whorl of teeth it used to slash at its prey. Male Falcatus sharks grew a huge spike over its head, for an unknown purpose.

Brush Head

Stethacanthus (≈360 mya)

Sharks survived a major extinction event at the end of the Devonian period that emptied the seas of many marine predators. So many new sharks with new features emerged during the Carboniferous period that it is sometimes called the "golden age of sharks." One of the new types of shark was *Stethacanthus*. It had a bristly, flat-topped fin jutting off the top of its head and also long "fin whips" trailing from its sides. Scientists are still trying to understand the purpose of these fins and theorize that they might have been used to attract mates or scare away predators.

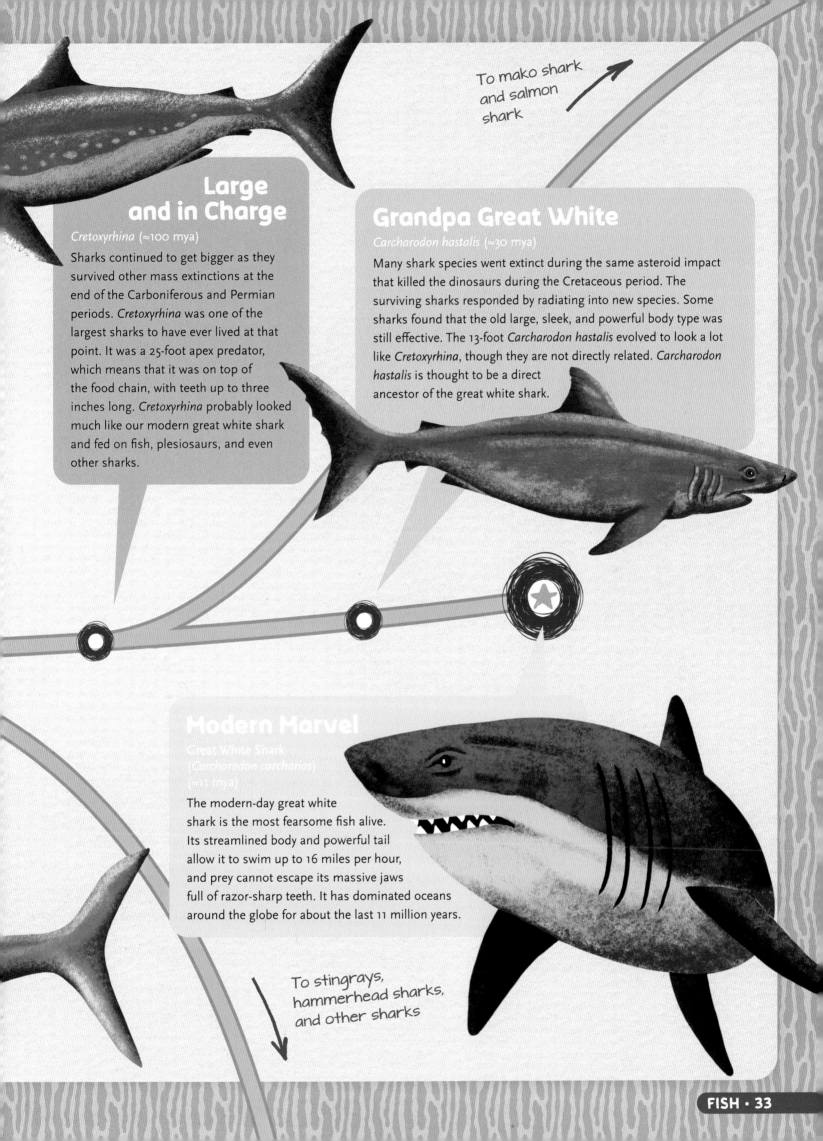

To mako shark and salmon shark

Large and in Charge

Cretoxyrhina (≈100 mya)

Sharks continued to get bigger as they survived other mass extinctions at the end of the Carboniferous and Permian periods. *Cretoxyrhina* was one of the largest sharks to have ever lived at that point. It was a 25-foot apex predator, which means that it was on top of the food chain, with teeth up to three inches long. *Cretoxyrhina* probably looked much like our modern great white shark and fed on fish, plesiosaurs, and even other sharks.

Grandpa Great White

Carcharodon hastalis (≈30 mya)

Many shark species went extinct during the same asteroid impact that killed the dinosaurs during the Cretaceous period. The surviving sharks responded by radiating into new species. Some sharks found that the old large, sleek, and powerful body type was still effective. The 13-foot *Carcharodon hastalis* evolved to look a lot like *Cretoxyrhina*, though they are not directly related. *Carcharodon hastalis* is thought to be a direct ancestor of the great white shark.

Modern Marvel

Great White Shark
(*Carcharodon carcharias*)
(~11 mya)

The modern-day great white shark is the most fearsome fish alive. Its streamlined body and powerful tail allow it to swim up to 16 miles per hour, and prey cannot escape its massive jaws full of razor-sharp teeth. It has dominated oceans around the globe for about the last 11 million years.

To stingrays, hammerhead sharks, and other sharks

A History of the Study of Evolution

For much of human history, ideas about the origins of plants and animals were derived from religious texts or oral traditions. But in the 18th and 19th centuries, scientists around the world began to develop new ideas based on evidence from fossils and from an increasing understanding of wildlife around the world.

Many scientists contributed to an understanding of evolution, but the most famous was an English naturalist named Charles Darwin. Darwin traveled the world between 1831 and 1836 aboard a research vessel, the HMS *Beagle*. During a stop at the Galapagos Islands off the west coast of Ecuador, Darwin noticed that much of the wildlife was similar to that on the South American mainland—giant tortoises, mockingbirds, and iguanas—but slightly different. He also noticed that there were slight differences between animals that lived on Galapagos Islands with different habitats.

When Darwin returned to England, he continued to study, converse with other scientists and naturalists, and develop his theory of evolution, first presented in his landmark 1859 book *On the Origin of Species*. The ideas of Darwin and his contemporaries were controversial because they contradicted what many people believed about the origins of life, but these ideas are now accepted as fundamental truths about the natural world. Still, new developments are being made all the time, and there is much about evolution and the history of particular species that we have still to learn.

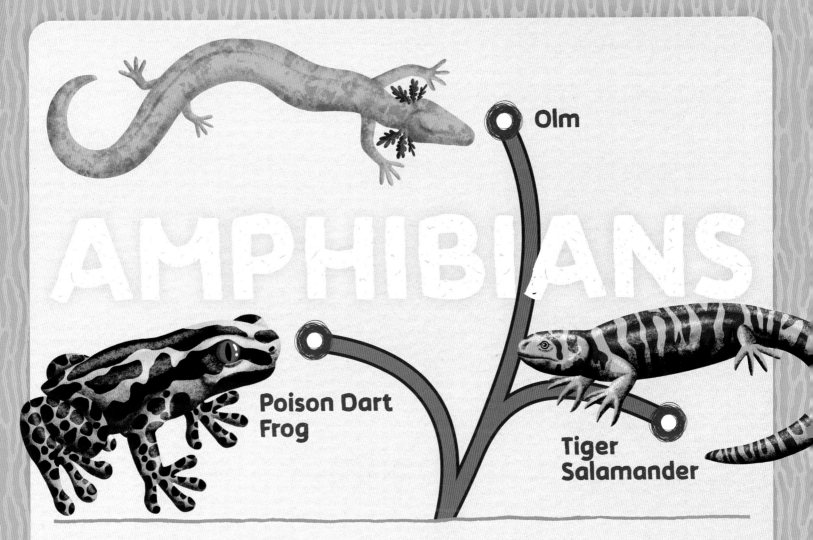

Olm

AMPHIBIANS

Poison Dart Frog

Tiger Salamander

T he story of amphibians begins with fish, which were evolving into all kinds of new forms in the Silurian and Devonian periods, more than 350 million years ago. One large group of fish were the "lobe-finned" fish, which had pairs of fleshy fins at the fronts and backs of their bodies that they used to push themselves along the seafloor. Some of these fish also developed lungs to help them breathe air when there was little oxygen in the water. Over many millions of years, some of those pushing fins evolved into limbs for walking, and lungs permitted the animals to breathe out of the water. These new animals, called tetrapods, were the first vertebrates to leave the water, and all other land-living vertebrates—amphibians, reptiles, mammals, and birds—would eventually evolve from them.

Most modern amphibians, which include frogs, salamanders, caecilians, and their relatives, hatch from eggs laid in fresh water, and many species stick close to water for their whole lives. Other amphibians have evolved to inhabit a variety of habitats, from jungles to arid deserts to the deepest, darkest caves. Three species of amphibians help explain how evolution brought these animals out of the water and onto—for the most part—dry land: the poison dart frog, the tiger salamander, and the olm.

POISON DART FROG

Frogs are the most famous and widespread of amphibians, with more than 5,000 known species around the world. From bullfrogs to tree frogs, from backyard ponds to jungle treetops, frogs' big eyes and hopping habits have endeared them to humans. However, not all frogs are so innocent. Poison dart frogs are famous for the deadly toxins they produce and for their brightly colored bodies, which serve as warnings to potential predators.

From the
Actinopterygii, page 29

Puddle Cruiser

Ichthyostega (≈360 mya)

By the late Devonian period, some lobe-finned fish sported bodies that would help them move between ponds or seek safety on land. *Ichthyostega* had four limbs that helped it move through shallow or swampy water. It also had a big, flat head and likely scooted around like a modern-day seal.

Taking a Hike

Temnospondyls (≈340 mya)

Temnospondyls were an early group of walking vertebrates that ventured from the water onto land to eat plants and insects. Temnospondyls were still mostly aquatic, but some, like *Phonerpeton*, might have spent nearly all their time on land, perhaps only returning to the water to lay eggs. Without competition from any other land vertebrates, temnospondyls were at the top of the terrestrial food chain in the Carboniferous period and are often considered the first amphibians.

A Sticky Situation

Some frogs have evolved long, sticky tongues that they can shoot out from their mouths at insects, helping them snag meals without having to move their bodies.

Better Bouncer

Prosalirus (≈180 mya)

As frogs continued to develop, they evolved a method to better hunt and escape predators: jumping. Strong hind legs with large, webbed feet allowed frogs like *Prosalirus* to leap upon unsuspecting insects and also to swim quickly away from danger.

To the reptiles, page 41, and the mammals, page 58

To bullfrogs, toads, and other frogs

Deadly Jewels

Poison Dart Frog (Dendrobatidae) (<65 mya)

Frogs diversified rapidly after the extinction of the dinosaurs 66 million years ago and eventually took their modern forms. One family that emerged is Dendrobatidae, or the poison dart frogs. These tropical frogs evolved their famously beautiful colors not to impress mates but to protect themselves! Poison dart frogs evolved to produce deadly toxins from the insects they eat, and their bright colors let potential predators know not to mess with them.

First Frog

Triadobatrachus (≈250 mya)

Triadobatrachus wasn't a large predator like its temnospondyl ancestors, mostly because reptiles had evolved over the past 100 million years and displaced amphibians at the top of the food chain. It had a very short tail and a bunch of extra bones in its back, which meant it wasn't officially a frog yet, but modern frogs were just a hop, skip, and a jump away—evolutionarily speaking, that is!

To the tiger salamander, page 38

Caution Colors

The development of bright colors for defense is called aposematism. Other examples from the animal kingdom include black-and-white skunks, whose coloration is a warning about their stinky spray, or the black-and-yellow coloration of bees and wasps.

TIGER SALAMANDER

Salamanders are most often encountered when they're walking on land on four legs, and they are sometimes mistaken for reptiles. But they're amphibians, like their cousins the frogs. Though seldom seen, there are hundreds of different species around the world, with bold and beautiful colors and patterns, varied body styles, and different hunting techniques.

Two species of salamanders, the tiger salamander and the olm, have evolved very different bodies that help them live in different habitats. Adult tiger salamanders walk along the forest floor hunting insects, slugs, and worms, while olms live only in pitch-black watery caves.

To the olm →

← From the temnospondyl, page 36

Starter Salamander

Marmorerpeton (≈167 mya)

Scientists have yet to find very many salamander fossils, and so there is a lot of debate about exactly when the creatures that became salamanders split away from the creatures that became frogs. But *Marmorerpeton*, from the Middle Jurassic, is considered one of the earliest salamanders and, like modern salamanders, likely looked for small prey in and out of the water.

Surf and Turf

Mole Salamander (≈125 mya)

Mole salamanders are born in the water and breathe by absorbing oxygen through gills growing outside of their bodies. However, when mole salamanders grow older, they leave the water and spend their time hunting insects and snails and staying safe in underground burrows. To help them breathe outside the water these salamanders have evolved to develop sets of internal lungs as adults.

Warning Signal

Tiger Salamander (*Ambystoma tigrinum*) (≈15 mya)

Tiger salamanders spend much of the day hiding in underground burrows and only emerge at night when it's easier to stay out of sight. Like their amphibian cousins the poison dart frogs, tiger salamanders evolved to become poisonous, and they have bright colors warning other animals to keep away.

Deep Breath

While tiger salamanders have developed lungs to breathe, many salamanders simply "breathe" air through their skin.

OLM

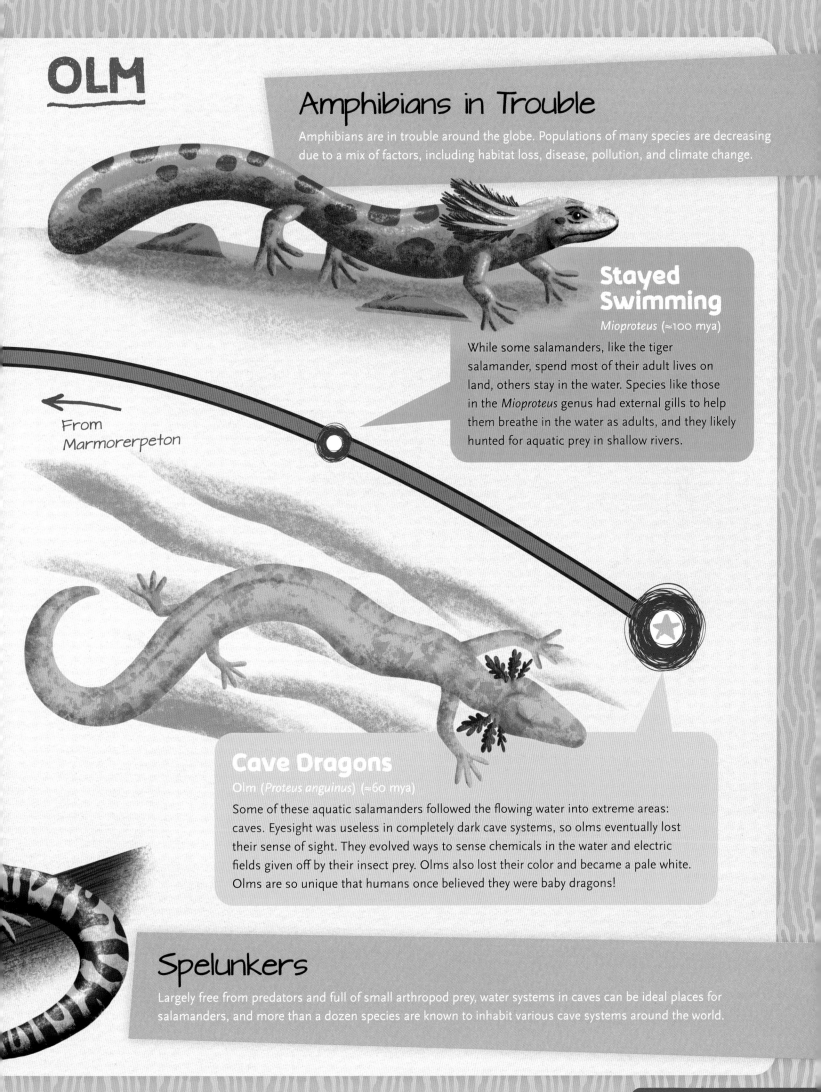

Amphibians in Trouble

Amphibians are in trouble around the globe. Populations of many species are decreasing due to a mix of factors, including habitat loss, disease, pollution, and climate change.

Stayed Swimming
Mioproteus (≈100 mya)

While some salamanders, like the tiger salamander, spend most of their adult lives on land, others stay in the water. Species like those in the *Mioproteus* genus had external gills to help them breathe in the water as adults, and they likely hunted for aquatic prey in shallow rivers.

From Marmorerpeton

Cave Dragons
Olm (*Proteus anguinus*) (≈60 mya)

Some of these aquatic salamanders followed the flowing water into extreme areas: caves. Eyesight was useless in completely dark cave systems, so olms eventually lost their sense of sight. They evolved ways to sense chemicals in the water and electric fields given off by their insect prey. Olms also lost their color and became a pale white. Olms are so unique that humans once believed they were baby dragons!

Spelunkers

Largely free from predators and full of small arthropod prey, water systems in caves can be ideal places for salamanders, and more than a dozen species are known to inhabit various cave systems around the world.

Convergent Evolution

Some features have evolved repeatedly throughout history in animals that are otherwise only distantly related, a phenomenon known as convergent evolution. When this occurs, species often evolve to look and behave alike.

One famous example of this effect is ichthyosaurs and dolphins. Ichthyosaurs were marine reptiles that cruised the oceans hunting fish more than 200 million years ago. Dolphins are modern-day mammals that also cruise the oceans hunting fish. Though their existences are separated by hundreds of millions of years, and one was a reptile and the other is a mammal, ichthyosaurs and dolphins look remarkably similar to each other. A sleek, streamlined body shape with a long snout full of sharp teeth is a successful body for a marine hunter, and both these animals evolved into it independently.

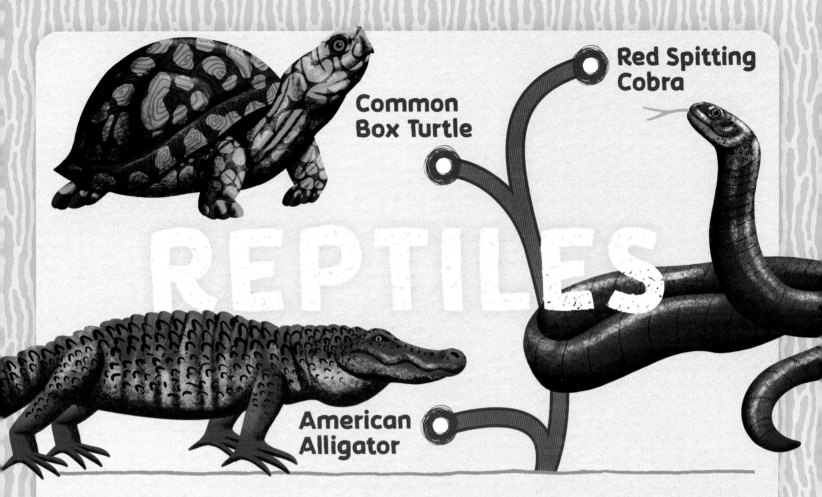

Common Box Turtle

Red Spitting Cobra

REPTILES

American Alligator

While some tetrapods remained tied to the water and evolved into amphibians, others adapted to leave the water behind entirely and became reptiles. The movement away from the water allowed reptiles to take many diverse forms and, for a while at least, rule Earth. The 184 million years of the Mesozoic era are known as the "age of the reptiles," the era when dinosaurs commanded the land, pterosaurs ruled the skies, and mosasaurs and plesiosaurs returned to dominate the seas.

The key development was the evolution of hard-shelled eggs, which meant that reptiles didn't need to lay their eggs in water as amphibians and fish did. Strong scales made of keratin—the same material that your fingernails are made of—gave reptiles a tough skin and protected them from the sun. These adaptations and others allowed reptiles to spend much more time on land than amphibians could and let them spread into drier habitats.

A large asteroid struck Earth 66 million years ago and caused worldwide destruction, eventually forcing many large reptile species to go extinct. But some of them survived, and the descendants of the world-conquering reptiles are still thriving around the globe. Three examples give a picture of how reptiles evolved to become such a diverse—sometimes deadly—group: the American alligator, the common box turtle, and the red spitting cobra.

AMERICAN ALLIGATOR

The modern order of Crocodilia contains more than 20 species of crocodiles, alligators, caimans, and other reptiles. Their large size and mouths full of sharp teeth helped crocodilians become some of the most formidable predators on Earth, and it's been that way for millions of years. Crocodilians can walk and lay eggs on land, but they hunt from the water.

Alligators have rounder, wider snouts than other crocodilians. The American alligator lives in freshwater wetlands and swamps throughout the southeastern United States, and it is a dominant predator, eating fish, mammals, and birds—and has even been known to attack humans. But it took millions of years for the earliest reptiles to evolve into our American alligators.

Leading Lizard

Hylonomus lyelli (≈315 mya)

The oldest true reptile that scientists have discovered is *Hylonomus lyelli*. It was a foot-long creature that looked surprisingly like a modern lizard. *Hylonomus lyelli* had sharp teeth and likely hunted insects.

Bigger and Badder

Proterosuchus (≈252 mya)

Reptiles were changing into different forms by the Late Permian. Some were growing bigger and developing stronger muscles in their bodies to make them faster. They were also developing lighter and more powerful jaws to become deadlier predators. *Proterosuchus* looked and likely behaved a lot like a modern crocodile: It was a powerful swimmer with a strong bite and a hooked snout. *Proterosuchus* was one of the earliest known archosauriforms, the group that eventually led to alligators, dinosaurs, and birds.

Speed Demon

Terrestrisuchus (≈200 mya)

Early members of the alligator family were successful predators, and many different species evolved. The two-foot-long *Terrestrisuchus* evolved long legs to help it chase down fast-moving prey along the tropical coastlines of what is now Great Britain.

To the mammals, page 58

To the common box turtle, page 44, and the red spitting cobra, page 46

To the chicken, page 50

Many Forms, All Hungry

Alligators aren't the only modern crocodilians left. Crocodiles look very similar to alligators, but they have pointed snouts and generally inhabit warmer waters. The Nile crocodile is one of the deadliest animals in Africa. Caimans are smaller and live in Central and South America, and gharials, from India, have evolved thinner snouts, perfect for snatching fish.

Dinosaur Hunter

Deinosuchus (≈82 mya)

While reptiles like *Terrestrisuchus* hunted on land, other early alligators returned to the water. Some of these evolved into ambush hunters. They'd wait motionless just below the surface at the water's edge and then pounce on unsuspecting animals coming for a drink. Long, powerful tails helped them swim and lunge. Huge jaws snapped down on escaping prey and held them tight. *Deinosuchus* looked very much like a modern crocodile or alligator, but it was about four times as large: up to 50 feet from snout to tail. Scientists believe that *Deinosuchus* had a stronger bite than any land animal in history, including the *Tyrannosaurus rex*, and it probably dined on large dinosaurs!

Modern Marvel

American Alligator (*Alligator mississippiensis*) (≈8 mya)

Most huge reptiles went extinct at the same time as the dinosaurs, but some crocodilians survived and still thrive today. The American alligator looks a lot like the mighty *Deinosuchus* did but is only about 12 feet long and preys on fish, amphibians, and small mammals. Despite their relatively smaller size, American alligators are the largest reptiles in the United States. They are found along the bayous and coastlines of the Southeast.

To crocodiles, caimans, and gharials

Vanishing Gators

Other than the American alligator, the world's only other living species of alligator is the critically endangered Chinese alligator, with fewer than 100 individuals left in the wild. The American alligator was in danger of going extinct in the mid-1900s, but protection under the Endangered Species Act has helped the reptile to a full recovery, with a current population estimated in the millions.

COMMON BOX TURTLE

A slow-moving animal like a turtle would make an easy meal for a predator if it hadn't evolved one of the most famous defenses of any animal: a shell. Bony shells give the ultimate protection for turtles and helped them become some of our most widespread and familiar reptiles. Turtles have moved into a variety of ecosystems, including most freshwater habitats, the open oceans (sea turtles), and even deserts (tortoises).

Dynamic Digger

Eunotosaurus (≈260 mya)

The evolutionary origins of turtle shells have long puzzled scientists, but some now believe that the earliest turtles evolved their shells not for defense, but for digging. *Eunotosaurus* had no shell, but it did have wide, flat ribs and powerful front claws. Scientists believe that its unusual rib cage helped anchor muscles that gave it a powerful digging stroke, perfect for a life spent in underground burrows in what is now South Africa.

From Hylonomus lyelli, page 42

Semishelled Reptile

Odontochelys (≈220 mya)

Odontochelys fossils were found with shells only covering these creatures' bellies but not their backs. Scientists are unsure whether they're finding just the bottom shells because the top shells had not yet evolved or if the top shells simply did not fossilize. They're also uncertain whether *Odontochelys* was using its bottom shell for digging, like *Eunotosaurus*, or for defense, like modern turtles.

Big Shells

The largest living sea turtle is the leatherback sea turtle, which can grow up to 7 feet long and weigh up to 1,500 pounds. The largest tortoises are the Galapagos tortoises, weighing nearly 1,000 pounds. However, the largest turtle known to science was the Archelon, a 15-foot, 4,900-pound sea turtle from the Late Cretaceous.

Fully Armored

Proganochelys (≈210 mya)

A bony shell was proving to be an evolutionary benefit, and turtles were fully shelled, armored tanks by the time of *Proganochelys*. Three-foot-long *Proganochelys* had a wide shell on top and bottom and had evolved spikes on its neck and tail for extra defense. *Proganochelys* was more turtle-like in other ways, too: While earlier turtles in the fossil record had lizard-like faces with jaws full of teeth, *Proganochelys* had a beak more like a modern turtle's, indicating that it was a herbivore.

Reinforcements!

A hard shell is not enough defense for some turtles. The mata mata turtle of South America has evolved elaborate camouflage: Its flattened head and bumpy shell look like leaves and bark lying on the riverbed, keeping the turtle safe from predators and allowing it to sneak up on and eat unsuspecting fish.

To sea turtles, sliders, tortoises, and others

Turtle Tank

Common Box Turtle
(*Terrapene carolina*) (≈2.5 mya)

One of the evolutionary trade-offs of having a large, bony shell is that all that armor makes walking difficult. Many turtles stick to the water, where they can avoid predators by swimming away, but turtles that spend a lot of time on land, like the common box turtle, need extra-secure protection. Unlike other turtles, the box turtle has a hinge on the bottom of its shell that closes up when the turtle pulls its head and limbs inside. The result is that the turtle becomes a hard "box," unable to be pried open by hungry predators. Their excellent defense has resulted in box turtles ranging all over North America.

RED SPITTING COBRA

Snakes are reptiles, but there is one very important difference between them and lizards, alligators, and turtles: Snakes lost their legs! The evolutionary history of snakes is a hotly debated topic among scientists, who are continually refining their theories about how, why, and when snakes lost their limbs based on new fossil evidence. But losing limbs hasn't stopped snakes from moving around—they can climb trees, burrow underground, and even swim—and becoming some of the world's most fearsome hunters. In addition to adaptations that make it a formidable offensive force, the four-foot-long red spitting cobra has evolved an incredible defense: When threatened, the snake can spit venom into the face of its attacker, causing major injuries or even death.

Early Lizard *Megachirella*

Megachirella (≈240 mya)

Megachirella is the oldest known of the Squamata, the group that led to lizards and snakes. It was a terrestrial lizard, perhaps similar in structure to an iguana. All reptiles are protected by tough, bony scales, and lizard scales evolved to overlap like roof tiles, preventing them from drying out in harsh environments like deserts.

← From *Hylonomus lyelli*, page 42

To iguanas, geckos, Komodo dragons, Gila monsters, and others

Small Spaces

Najash (≈90 mya)

Many reptiles use underground burrows to seek shelter from the hot sun or to hunt for food. Reptiles that live in underground burrows have independently evolved to lose their limbs over the millions of years they've been on Earth. One of those reptiles—*Najash* from the Late Cretaceous—still had hind legs, but they were very small. Lizards with smaller limbs and long, smooth bodies could more easily fit through tight spaces; they were becoming snakes.

Improved Hunter

Dinilysia (≈85 mya)

Finding food in the underground darkness is difficult, and so any advantage that helped snakes get a meal was likely to be passed along. Eventually, snakes evolved special bones in their heads to help them "hear" the vibrations of the world around them through the ground, a trait that modern snakes rely on as stealthy hunters. At nearly six feet long, *Dinilysia* was one of the largest of the early snakes. It hunted in what is now South America.

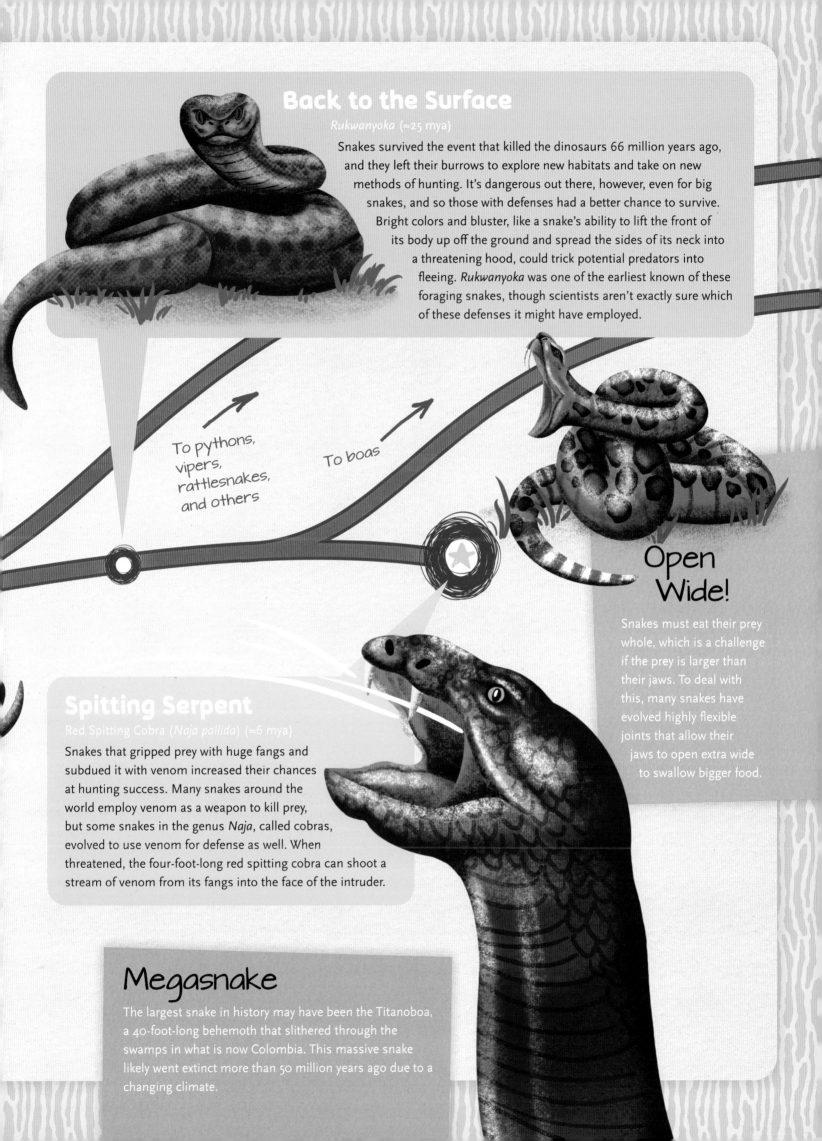

Back to the Surface

Rukwanyoka (≈25 mya)

Snakes survived the event that killed the dinosaurs 66 million years ago, and they left their burrows to explore new habitats and take on new methods of hunting. It's dangerous out there, however, even for big snakes, and so those with defenses had a better chance to survive. Bright colors and bluster, like a snake's ability to lift the front of its body up off the ground and spread the sides of its neck into a threatening hood, could trick potential predators into fleeing. *Rukwanyoka* was one of the earliest known of these foraging snakes, though scientists aren't exactly sure which of these defenses it might have employed.

To pythons, vipers, rattlesnakes, and others

To boas

Open Wide!

Snakes must eat their prey whole, which is a challenge if the prey is larger than their jaws. To deal with this, many snakes have evolved highly flexible joints that allow their jaws to open extra wide to swallow bigger food.

Spitting Serpent

Red Spitting Cobra (*Naja pallida*) (≈6 mya)

Snakes that gripped prey with huge fangs and subdued it with venom increased their chances at hunting success. Many snakes around the world employ venom as a weapon to kill prey, but some snakes in the genus *Naja*, called cobras, evolved to use venom for defense as well. When threatened, the four-foot-long red spitting cobra can shoot a stream of venom from its fangs into the face of the intruder.

Megasnake

The largest snake in history may have been the Titanoboa, a 40-foot-long behemoth that slithered through the swamps in what is now Colombia. This massive snake likely went extinct more than 50 million years ago due to a changing climate.

Extinction

"Extinction" is the term for when a kind of living thing ceases to exist. The vast majority of species that have existed on Earth are no longer alive today. Dinosaurs, pterosaurs, trilobites, cave bears, mammoths, and millions of other animals, plants, and other life forms have, at some point in Earth's history, evolved, flourished, and then completely disappeared. Most will have come and gone without humans ever learning of their existence.

Species go extinct for many reasons. Sometimes it can happen relatively quickly. The most famous example of this occurred when an asteroid hit Earth 66 million years ago. The worldwide damage in the aftermath of the impact was so catastrophic that many species quickly went extinct, including dinosaurs.

Extinction can also occur gradually. Over time a species' habitat might change such that they can no longer survive, or they may become outcompeted by another species.

Sword-Billed Hummingbird

BIRDS

Kākāpō

Chicken

While the dinosaurs were stomping around on the ground, gigantic reptiles called pterosaurs were soaring through the air on wings made of skin stretched between long modified fingers. Scientists know of more than 100 different species of pterosaurs, including *Quetzalcoatlus*, which—with a wingspan of 30 feet—is the largest known flying animal of all time.

But at the same time that pterosaurs were soaring through the skies, a group of dinosaurs were evolving to fly in a different way—certain dinosaurs were evolving feathers. Feathers may have evolved first to help keep reptiles warm, or perhaps to show off to potential mates, but eventually dinosaurs began using them to fly.

Early feathered dinosaurs may have just used their feathers to glide from tree to tree because their bones made them too heavy to do much more. But these dinosaurs continued to evolve, becoming lighter. They lost their heavy, bony tails. Their reptile jaws evolved into lightweight beaks. Eventually, perhaps around 150 million years ago, these dinosaurs were no longer dinosaurs at all; they were birds.

The asteroid impact 66 million years ago devastated Mesozoic life. The giant flying pterosaurs all went extinct, and so did the dinosaurs. But, somehow, some birds survived and flourished, evolving into many different shapes and sizes to help them survive in nearly every habitat on Earth.

CHICKEN

Believe it or not, the clucking little barnyard chicken has a fearsome ancestry: It descends from dinosaurs. One group of dinosaurs called the theropods, which included the legendary *Tyrannosaurus rex*, evolved to walk on two legs, freeing up their arms to use for grasping and, millions of years later, for flying. And these dinosaurs had another special adaptation: They evolved thin, tubular feathers, which likely helped keep them warm.

The path from theropod to chicken saw dinosaurs evolving into birds. Then emerged a branch that was made up of stocky, mostly ground-dwelling birds called Galliformes, which today includes modern pheasants, turkeys, grouse, and others. Then humans got involved, guiding the evolution of a wild pheasant into our domestic chicken, the most numerous bird on Earth.

To the sword-billed hummingbird, page 52, and the kākāpō, page 54, and other birds

Dinosaur Kings

Theropods (≈240 mya)

The theropods began as a group of carnivorous dinosaurs that walked on two legs, hunting and scavenging throughout the Triassic, Jurassic, and Cretaceous periods. The earliest theropods, like the dog-sized *Eodromaeus*, arose during the Late Triassic and likely hunted small reptiles and insects. The most famous theropod dinosaur is the *Tyrannosaurus rex*, a 40-foot-long creature known as one of the fiercest predators of all time. T. rex was a theropod and so are modern birds, but the lines leading from theropod ancestors to T. rex and birds had split long before T. rex itself evolved.

Losing Weight

Confuciusornis (≈127 mya)

The lighter a dinosaur was, the easier it was to fly. *Confuciusornis* had evolved long tail feathers that took the place of a bony reptile tail and had replaced its heavy, bony jaws and teeth with a strong, light beak.

From *Proterosuchus*, page 42

Feathered Dinosaur

Archaeopteryx (≈150 mya)

Archaeopteryx was the earliest known dinosaur to have modified feathers used for gliding. *Archaeopteryx* fossils show that some of their feathers had special barbs that could "zip" together to form a rigid surface for flying—just like the flight feathers of modern birds. *Archaeopteryx* hadn't evolved the muscles that would allow it to fly powerfully, so it likely just glided between trees. Only about the size of a modern crow, *Archaeopteryx* hunted along tropical seas during the Jurassic period.

To Tyrannosaurus rex

Out of Sight

Ptarmigans are Galliformes that live on the Arctic tundra, where there is little to keep them hidden. To help them stay out of sight of predators like gyrfalcons and arctic foxes, ptarmigans have evolved camouflage plumage: white feathers in the winter to match the snow and a mix of reds and browns to match summer vegetation.

Back on the Ground

Gallinuloides wyomingensis (≈48 mya)

Scientists aren't precisely sure where dinosaurs stopped and birds began, but there were certainly birds on Earth during the Cretaceous. One group was the Galliformes, which are believed to have existed at least 80 million years ago. They were birds with short, strong legs that spent much of their time walking and feeding on seeds and other vegetation on the ground and using their wings only when necessary to escape predators.

Docile Dinosaur

Chicken (≈8,000 years ago)

Red jungle fowl were domesticated thousands of years ago, likely in Southeast Asia. Humans have since guided their evolution, breeding chickens into many different shapes, sizes, and colors. Chickens are an important food source around the globe, and most of today's domestic chickens have been bred to be larger and more docile than their wild cousins. There are an estimated 23 billion chickens alive on Earth at any given time, making them a far more numerous species than humans.

Wild Chicken

Red Jungle Fowl (≈5 mya)

The Galliformes were a successful order of birds, with many modern relatives, including grouse, ptarmigans, pheasants, quails, and more. The red jungle fowl is a modern-day Galliformes, found in Southeast Asia. Male red jungle fowl have evolved bright colors, bold fleshy crests, and long tail feathers, and they announce their presence with a loud "cock-a-doodle-doo!"—all features that are necessary to help them attract mates!

To turkeys, ducks, geese, and more

SWORD-BILLED HUMMINGBIRD

The sword-billed hummingbird is simply one of the most incredible birds on Earth. Hummingbirds are the only type of bird that has evolved to fly backward and upside down. Those traits evolved to help it hover in front of flowers. The sword-billed hummingbird evolved a massive bill to help it drink nectar from long flowers. It's so long, in fact, that the sword-billed hummingbird is the only bird on the planet with a bill longer than its body.

To swifts and tree swifts

← From *Confuciusornis*, page 50

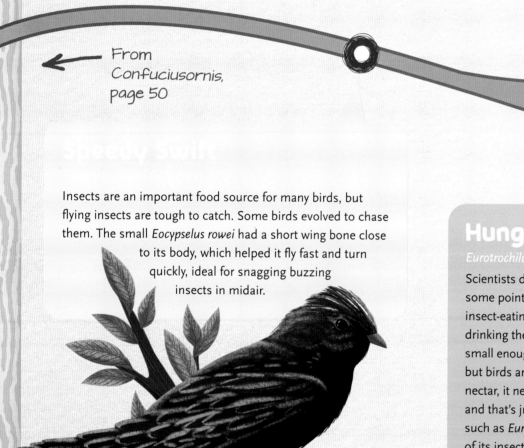

Speedy Swift

Insects are an important food source for many birds, but flying insects are tough to catch. Some birds evolved to chase them. The small *Eocypselus rowei* had a short wing bone close to its body, which helped it fly fast and turn quickly, ideal for snagging buzzing insects in midair.

Hungry Hoverers
Eurotrochilus (≈30 mya)

Scientists don't know exactly how or when, but at some point, the descendants of those fast-flying, insect-eating birds expanded their diets and began drinking the nectar of flowers. Insects like bees are small enough to simply land on flowers and drink, but birds are too heavy. If a bird wants to drink nectar, it needs to hover in front of the flower, and that's just what the earliest hummingbirds, such as *Eurotrochilus*, could do. The quick wings of its insect-eating ancestors evolved further to include special joints that rotated in all directions, giving these early hummingbirds ultimate control in midair. *Eurotrochilus* fossils from what is now Germany reveal that hummingbirds existed at least 30 million years ago.

Bird or Insect?

Hummingbirds must beat their wings extremely quickly—as many as 80 beats per second—in order to hover, and all that beating requires a lot of energy. Hummingbirds need to eat almost constantly to have enough energy to fly, and most have evolved very small, light bodies that are relatively easy to keep in the air. The smallest hummingbird of all, and the smallest bird on Earth, is the bee hummingbird of Cuba, which is less than three inches long.

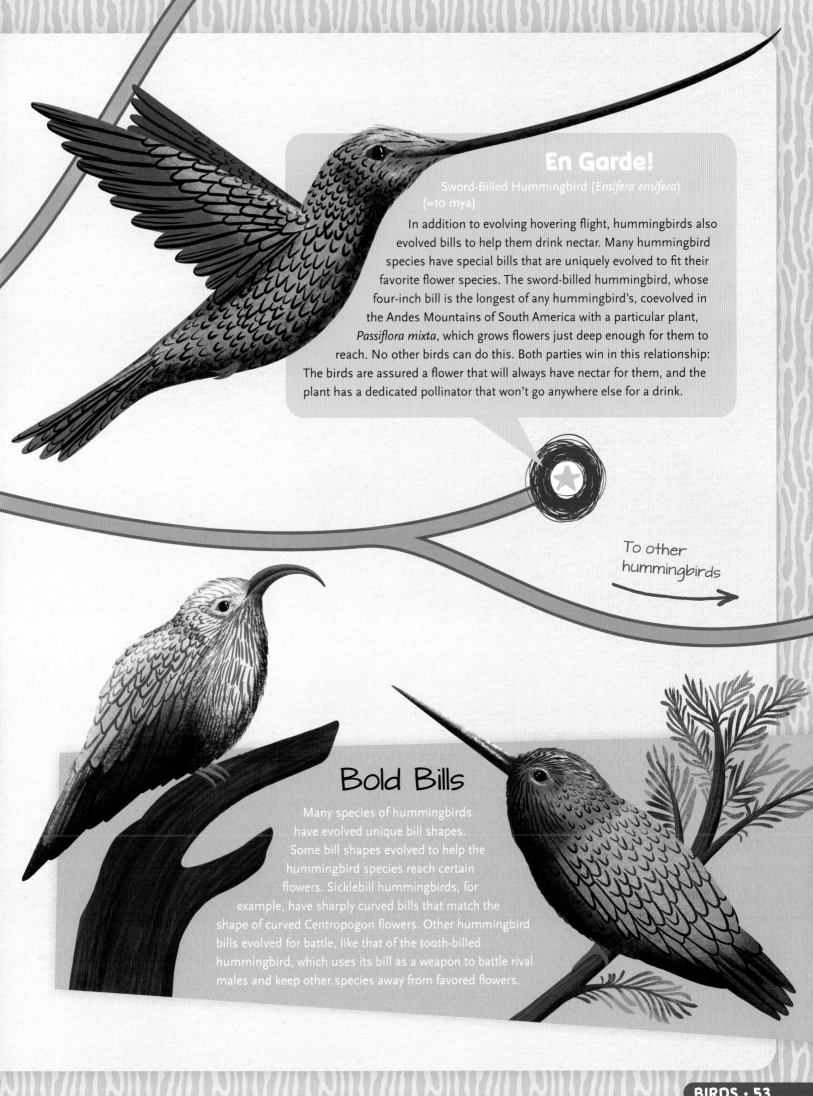

En Garde!

Sword-Billed Hummingbird (*Ensifera ensifera*)
(≈10 mya)

In addition to evolving hovering flight, hummingbirds also evolved bills to help them drink nectar. Many hummingbird species have special bills that are uniquely evolved to fit their favorite flower species. The sword-billed hummingbird, whose four-inch bill is the longest of any hummingbird's, coevolved in the Andes Mountains of South America with a particular plant, *Passiflora mixta*, which grows flowers just deep enough for them to reach. No other birds can do this. Both parties win in this relationship: The birds are assured a flower that will always have nectar for them, and the plant has a dedicated pollinator that won't go anywhere else for a drink.

To other hummingbirds

Bold Bills

Many species of hummingbirds have evolved unique bill shapes. Some bill shapes evolved to help the hummingbird species reach certain flowers. Sicklebill hummingbirds, for example, have sharply curved bills that match the shape of curved Centropogon flowers. Other hummingbird bills evolved for battle, like that of the tooth-billed hummingbird, which uses its bill as a weapon to battle rival males and keep other species away from favored flowers.

KĀKĀPŌ

The unique natural history of New Zealand has led to some unusual animal evolutions. Mammals had not yet reached New Zealand when it began breaking away from Australia some 85 million years ago, and so the animals that did make it had to fly or swim.

Parrots made their way to New Zealand from Australia. Parrots living elsewhere in the world are often brightly colored, loud, and strong fliers. But in a land without mammals, the kākāpō evolved to become flightless, nocturnal, land-dwelling herbivores. Though related to flashy parrots in the rest of the world, the kākāpō and its incredible path reveal how powerful evolution can be.

To macaws, cockatoos, lorikeets, and more

From Confuciusornis, page 50

To falcons and others

Terrifying Terror Bird
Cretaceous Bird of Prey (≈85 mya)

Though no fossils have been found, scientists studying genetic data believe that a meat-eating bird evolved during the age of the dinosaurs. They believe it was a predator with a hooked beak and strong talons, adaptations the bird used to grasp prey and tear flesh. Scientists have dubbed the extinct predators "terror birds."

Going Nuts
Cenozoic Psittacine (≈60 mya)

Some of these predatory birds survived the Cretaceous-Paleogene extinction, and some of their descendants began to feed on large seeds and nuts that appeared in the Cenozoic era. These birds evolved very strong and maneuverable bills to help them crack tough seeds. These birds were the first parrots, and their large, curved bills remain modern parrots' most useful tool.

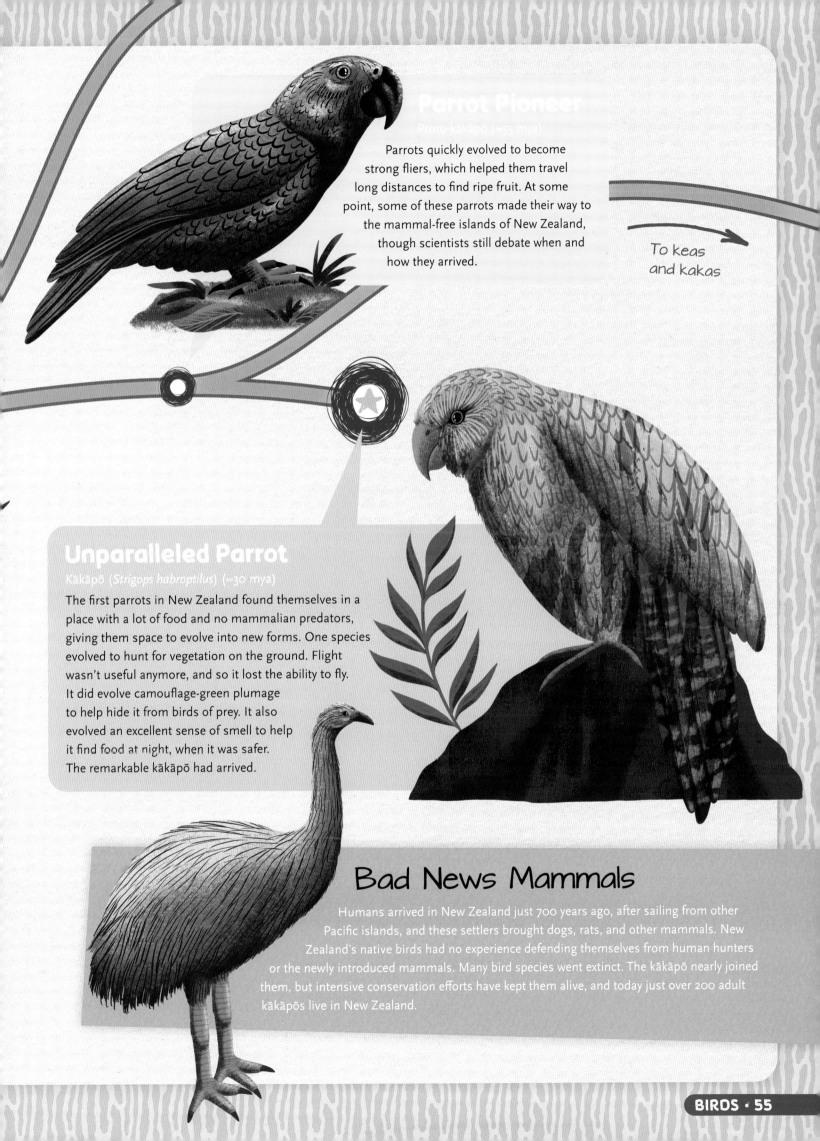

Parrot Pioneer
Proto-kākāpō (≈55 mya)

Parrots quickly evolved to become strong fliers, which helped them travel long distances to find ripe fruit. At some point, some of these parrots made their way to the mammal-free islands of New Zealand, though scientists still debate when and how they arrived.

To keas and kakas

Unparalleled Parrot
Kākāpō (*Strigops habroptilus*) (≈30 mya)

The first parrots in New Zealand found themselves in a place with a lot of food and no mammalian predators, giving them space to evolve into new forms. One species evolved to hunt for vegetation on the ground. Flight wasn't useful anymore, and so it lost the ability to fly. It did evolve camouflage-green plumage to help hide it from birds of prey. It also evolved an excellent sense of smell to help it find food at night, when it was safer. The remarkable kākāpō had arrived.

Bad News Mammals

Humans arrived in New Zealand just 700 years ago, after sailing from other Pacific islands, and these settlers brought dogs, rats, and other mammals. New Zealand's native birds had no experience defending themselves from human hunters or the newly introduced mammals. Many bird species went extinct. The kākāpō nearly joined them, but intensive conservation efforts have kept them alive, and today just over 200 adult kākāpōs live in New Zealand.

Cretaceous-Paleogene Extinction

Dinosaurs ruled Earth for more than 170 million years, but their reign came to an abrupt and terrifying end. One day 66 million years ago, a nine-mile-wide asteroid smashed into what is now Mexico. The impact caused a shock wave and tsunamis that destroyed plant and animal life for thousands of miles around. Earth's temperature spiked as billions of tons of debris kicked into the air by the impact began to rain.

Scientists estimate that 75 percent of all life on Earth went extinct as a result of the asteroid impact. However, 25 percent of life survived and eventually emerged into a totally new world. Many species of insects, fish, reptiles, amphibians, and birds survived, and their ancestors are still around today. Mammals, which had been tiny and nocturnal—necessary to hide from predatory dinosaurs—were able to emerge from their burrows and eventually take over the world.

Humans Can Guide Evolution

Humans can sometimes guide evolution by selecting which combinations and mutations they want to move forward. For example, the ancestor of our common barnyard sheep was a wild sheep from Europe and Asia called a mouflon. Wild mouflon are large, with huge curved horns and short dark brown coats. After humans began raising mouflon for meat and skins, they would select mouflon with the traits they liked, such as thicker coats or calmer temperaments, and let them breed. After many generations of humans breeding mouflon babies with the traits they wanted, the mouflon changed from long-horned, short-haired wild sheep to the gentle, chubby sheep with the thick white coats we know today.

Humans have influenced the evolution of all kinds of things, oftentimes causing huge transformations. Humans domesticated wolves and guided their evolution over generations into hundreds of different breeds of dogs. We did the same for cats (which used to be wildcats), chickens (which used to be jungle birds), and lots of fruits and vegetables (wild bananas have big, huge seeds!). In each of these cases, humans allowed wild things to breed, chose the offspring with the most desirable traits, and allowed them to reproduce.

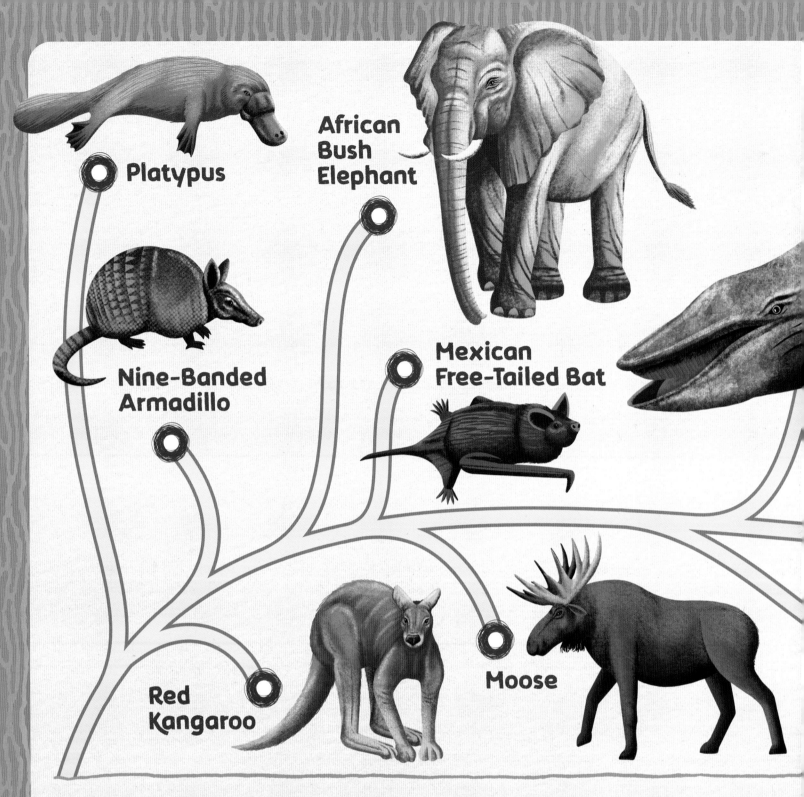

Platypus

African Bush Elephant

Nine-Banded Armadillo

Mexican Free-Tailed Bat

Red Kangaroo

Moose

If you're reading this book, you're a mammal. The bodies we mammals have evolved over hundreds of millions of years can look very different from species to species, but they have a few things in common. We all have hair or fur. We all give birth to live babies (with the exception of the monotremes, see page 60), and we all nourish those babies with milk.

But mammals didn't start out looking anything like humans. Instead, we looked a lot like reptiles. There was an important split among early egg-laying animals during the Carboniferous, about 315 million years ago. Creatures like *Hylonomus lyelli* (see page 42) went one way and became reptiles. Creatures called synapsids

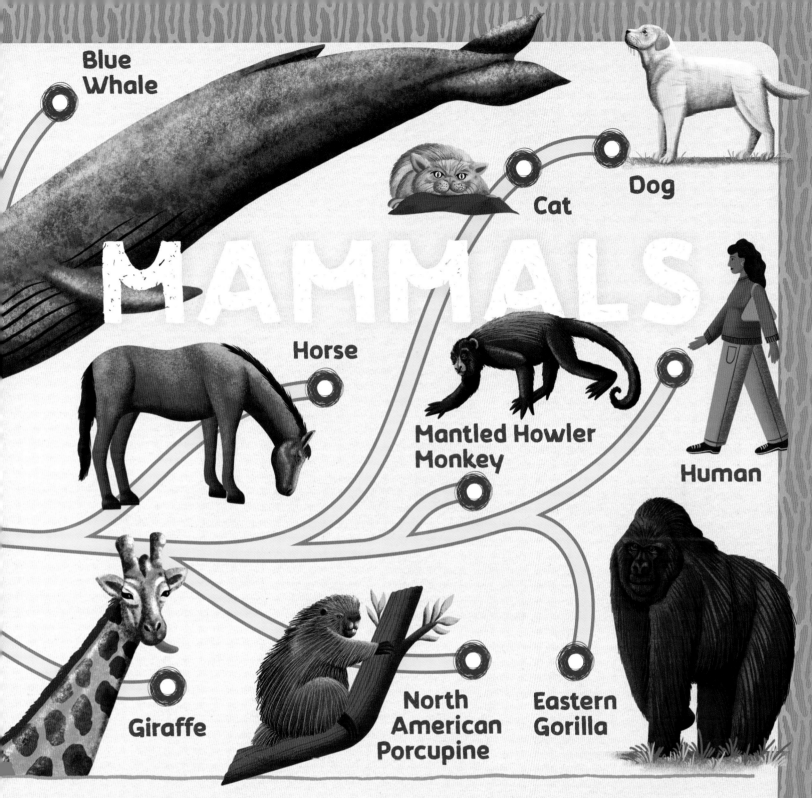

Blue Whale

Cat

Dog

Horse

Mantled Howler Monkey

Human

Giraffe

North American Porcupine

Eastern Gorilla

MAMMALS

went another way and eventually became mammals.

Reptiles and the earliest mammals continued to evolve side by side, but the need to stay safe from dinosaurs and other reptiles helped drive the evolution of mammals. When the dinosaurs went extinct, mammals fared relatively well.

The Cenozoic era, the period spanning the extinction of the dinosaurs 66 million years ago until today, is also known as the "age of the mammals." Mammals have been able to radiate into many different forms, from extinct beasts like *Megatherium* and saber-toothed cats to living mammals like elephants, whales, and humans.

PLATYPUS

Monotremes are the only mammals that lay eggs. They share this trait with birds and reptiles, and they have certain bones and other features that reptiles have but other mammals don't. Because of these two things, scientists believe the monotremes split from other mammals earlier than any other living group.

The most famous living monotreme is the platypus. European scientists were dumbfounded when they were first presented with platypus specimens in the late 1700s—they'd never seen a creature with fur like a mouse but with webbed feet and a bill like a duck. They thought it must have been a hoax, but in fact the platypus is simply a marvel of evolution.

Meet the Mammals

Megazostrodon (≈200 mya)

As with most of the earliest mammals, the most important thing for *Megazostrodon* was staying safe from hungry dinosaurs. This small mouselike creature likely spent its days hiding in underground burrows and its nights out hunting insects. *Megazostrodon* had evolved strong senses of smell and hearing to help it find food in the dark. It also may have had sensitive hairs near its mouth—whiskers—to help it feel its dark surroundings. Dating from the Late Triassic, *Megazostrodon* is considered to be one of the first true mammals.

To echidnas

From the tetrapods, page 41

An Early Offshoot

Teinolophos (≈120 mya)

Not much is known about *Teinolophos*. It was only about four inches long and likely ate insects and small invertebrates. Still, scientists studying the fossilized teeth of *Teinolophos* recognize their shape as being that of the monotremes and not of other types of mammals. And that means the platypus had already split off during the age of the dinosaurs.

To the rest of the mammals

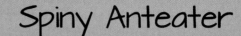

Spiny Anteater

The only other living monotreme is the echidna. Four echidna species remain in Australia and Papua New Guinea, and though they are the closest living relatives of the platypus, they look nothing alike. In a similar evolution to porcupines, echidnas evolved spines on their backs for defense, and they walk through forests looking for ants and termites.

Underwater Adaptations

Obdurodon (≈24 mya)

Nearly 100 million years later, one branch of the monotremes led to *Obdurodon*, a nearly three-foot-long mammal with a body evolved to help it catch aquatic prey. It may have hunted like a crocodile, floating quietly at the surface of the water. When it spotted a potential meal, *Obdurodon*'s webbed feet propelled it quickly through the water, and it snapped up prey in its wide, flat skin-covered snout, which had evolved for maximum scooping.

Dynamic Diver

Platypus (*Ornithorhynchus anatinus*) (≈1 mya)

Obdurodon died out for unknown reasons, but a close relative still swims in the streams and ponds of eastern Australia today: the platypus. The platypus has evolved to find food at the bottom of the pond instead of at the surface. Finding prey hidden under rocks at the bottom of a murky pond is a challenge, so the platypus's bill is equipped with special sensors made for electroreception, which is the ability to sense the minute electric fields given off by the worms, shrimp, and other animals it eats.

Venomous Mammals?

Another of the platypus's amazing adaptations is that it is one of only a few mammals to produce venom. Male platypuses can inject venom from bony spurs behind their ankles, useful for fighting with other males and perhaps fending off predators like crocodiles.

RED KANGAROO

Marsupials are a group of mammals that do not lay eggs. Instead, they evolved to let their babies grow inside their mothers' bodies before they are born. One benefit of this adaptation is that the developing baby goes wherever the mother goes, so the parents aren't tied to a specific nesting spot. Babies carried by the mother can also receive constant nourishment instead of being sealed off in an egg. But baby marsupials are born before they can fend for themselves and so stay with their mothers while they continue to develop. When it's born, a tiny baby marsupial instinctively crawls inside a special pouch on its mother's body. Inside, it is safe and warm and continues to grow by drinking the milk produced by its mother. After a few months, the baby is big enough to leave the pouch and live on its own.

Marsupials dominate the island of Australia, and millions of years of isolation have helped kangaroos, koalas, wombats, and other marsupials evolve into some of the most unusual and interesting mammals on Earth.

From mammals, page 58 ←

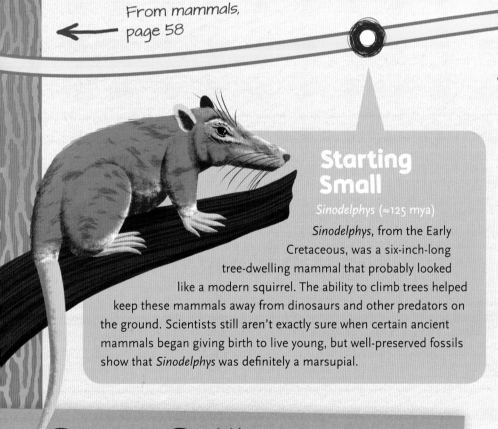

Starting Small

Sinodelphys (≈125 mya)

Sinodelphys, from the Early Cretaceous, was a six-inch-long tree-dwelling mammal that probably looked like a modern squirrel. The ability to climb trees helped keep these mammals away from dinosaurs and other predators on the ground. Scientists still aren't exactly sure when certain ancient mammals began giving birth to live young, but well-preserved fossils show that *Sinodelphys* was definitely a marsupial.

Spreading South

Microbiotheria (≈55 mya)

After the dinosaurs went extinct, marsupials branched out into different groups, including Microbiotheria. Species in this group of tiny tree-dwelling creatures looked like a cross between a mouse, a monkey, and an opossum. They lived primarily in what is now South America, but scientists recognize Microbiotheres as being the ancestors of the explosion of marsupial evolution that occurred on another continent: Australia.

Bounce Battle

Kangaroos live in groups, and males often fight one another over females, for access to food, and to determine social status. To fight, kangaroos often lean back on their strong, thick tails and kick at each other with both feet.

Hopped Up

Nambaroo (≈25 mya)

Australia's climate dried out in the Oligocene, turning forests into grasslands and forcing tree-dwelling mammals to adapt to life on the ground. *Nambaroo* were a group of early kangaroos that are believed to have both climbed in trees and walked on the ground. *Nambaroo* likely walked on all fours, but later kangaroos needed a more efficient method of traveling long distances between food sources: hopping. Eventually, the ancestors of modern kangaroos evolved long, elastic tendons in their hind legs, which acted like pogo sticks and allowed them to bound across the outback.

Pouched Tiger

While most of the carnivorous marsupials died off long ago, the thylacine, or Tasmanian tiger, survived until 1933. This beautiful dog-sized animal had stripes running down its back and tail, thought to act as camouflage as it hunted in woodlands.

To wallabies, eastern gray
kangaroos, tree kangaroos,
and others

Big Bouncer

Red Kangaroo (≈2 mya)

The earliest kangaroos, like *Nambaroo*, proved successful on the Australian grasslands, and many types of kangaroos evolved in the following years. *Propleopus* ate meat, unlike any other known kangaroo, and at over 6 feet tall and 240 pounds, *Procoptodon* was the largest kangaroo known to science. Many prehistoric kangaroos died out due to various environmental changes in Australia and from human impacts. The largest living kangaroo is the red kangaroo, which can stand 6 feet tall and weighs nearly 200 pounds. These kangaroos are found throughout the arid regions of central Australia, feeding on grasses and hopping at speeds up to 35 miles per hour. They bounce 6 feet off the ground and cover 25 feet in a single leap!

To wombats, koalas,
Tasmanian devils,
and others

NINE-BANDED ARMADILLO

The young of placental mammals develop inside their mothers' bodies. Babies of placental mammals are nourished inside their mothers through an organ called the placenta, which serves to provide nutrition and oxygen to the developing baby while also removing waste. When the young are finally born, they are relatively larger, more mature, and better able to survive on their own than marsupial babies. Early placental mammals were generally more successful than marsupials, and placental mammals are the most common type of mammal today everywhere except Australia. Placental mammals have diversified into many different forms, from flying bats to undersea whales and many things in between.

One placental mammal with unique evolutionary adaptations is the armadillo. Many animals have evolved ways to protect themselves, from spines to poison to camouflage. Armadillos have evolved armor. These tiny tanks live throughout South America, with just one species, the nine-banded armadillo, making its way north into the United States.

Tiny Hunter

Juramaia (≈160 mya)

Juramaia is the oldest presumed placental mammal known. Like so many mammals in the age of the dinosaurs, *Juramaia* was a small shrewlike animal that hunted insects from trees in the Late Jurassic.

Protective Shell

Utaetus (≈40 mya)

A group of mammals called Xenarthra separated early on from the rest of the placental mammals and evolved in isolation in what is now South America. Some xenarthrans were specialized to eat insects, featuring strong claws for digging into ant nests and termite mounds. But lumbering along the ground hunting insects leaves mammals vulnerable to predators, and so some evolved armor. Flat tiles of bone evolved to grow from the skin and cover the animals' bodies, giving them strong, turtle-like shells for protection, and they became armadillos. *Utaetus* is the earliest known, from the Eocene epoch, and is thought to have looked much like a modern armadillo.

Large and Small

The massive *Glyptodon* and other huge species died out thousands of years ago, and the world's current largest armadillo species is the three-foot-long giant armadillo of northeastern South America. The smallest living species is the five-inch-long pink fairy armadillo, which lives belowground in Argentina.

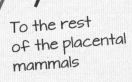

To the rest
of the placental
mammals

Slow and Steady

Another major group of xenarthrans is the sloths, which use their huge claws not for digging but for hanging on to branches as they eat leaves. Modern sloths are famous for moving incredibly slowly, using their stillness and shaggy bodies as camouflage to hide from potential predators as they slowly digest leaves.

Mega Tank

Glyptodon (≈2 mya)

Some xenarthrans, animals in the group of South American mammals that included *Utaetus*, grew to massive size. One branch of the family is the sloths, and the Early Pliocene ground sloth *Megatherium* grew as large as an elephant. *Glyptodon* was part of another branch. It was a huge relative of modern armadillos, with a dome-shaped shell the size of a small car that it used to fend off saber-toothed cats and dire wolves. Humans lived alongside *Glyptodon* and likely hunted it for food.

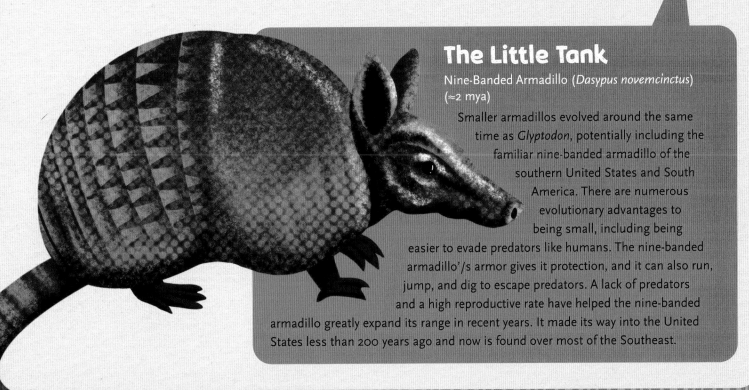

The Little Tank

Nine-Banded Armadillo (*Dasypus novemcinctus*)
(≈2 mya)

Smaller armadillos evolved around the same time as *Glyptodon*, potentially including the familiar nine-banded armadillo of the southern United States and South America. There are numerous evolutionary advantages to being small, including being easier to evade predators like humans. The nine-banded armadillo'/s armor gives it protection, and it can also run, jump, and dig to escape predators. A lack of predators and a high reproductive rate have helped the nine-banded armadillo greatly expand its range in recent years. It made its way into the United States less than 200 years ago and now is found over most of the Southeast.

AFRICAN BUSH ELEPHANT

African elephants are the largest land animals alive today. They are beloved creatures, admired for their wisdom, kindness, and strength. An elephant's most prominent feature is its long trunk, which evolved from the flexible lip of its ancestors. They have huge ears to help them keep cool and huge tusks to help them dig for food and defend themselves. The origins of these massive beasts stretch back millions of years, when their ancestors looked much different.

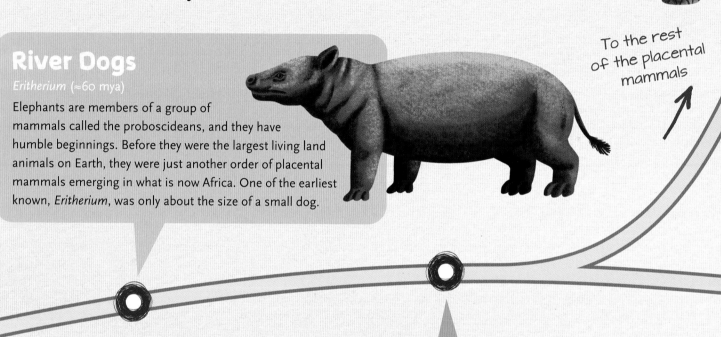

River Dogs
Eritherium (≈60 mya)

Elephants are members of a group of mammals called the proboscideans, and they have humble beginnings. Before they were the largest living land animals on Earth, they were just another order of placental mammals emerging in what is now Africa. One of the earliest known, *Eritherium*, was only about the size of a small dog.

To the rest of the placental mammals

Big-Mouthed "Beast"
Moeritherium (≈37 mya)

The "beast of Lake Moeris" was found on a dry lake bed in Egypt, which enjoyed a wet, tropical climate during the Eocene. *Moeritherium* was bigger than *Eritherium*, but it still looked more like a small hippopotamus than an elephant. However, scientists believe that it may have had a flexible upper lip that helped it grab aquatic vegetation—the beginnings of the famous elephant trunk had appeared.

Conquering the Cold

A famous extinct relative of modern elephants, the woolly mammoth lived in the cold regions of what is now northern North America and Russia. We have an excellent understanding of what they looked like from cave paintings of early humans and frozen specimens dug from the Arctic. About the size of modern living elephants, woolly mammoths evolved long coats of brown hair to keep them warm in freezing temperatures and massive, curved tusks. Unlike modern elephants, which have large ears to help radiate heat, woolly mammoths had small ears to help prevent frostbite.

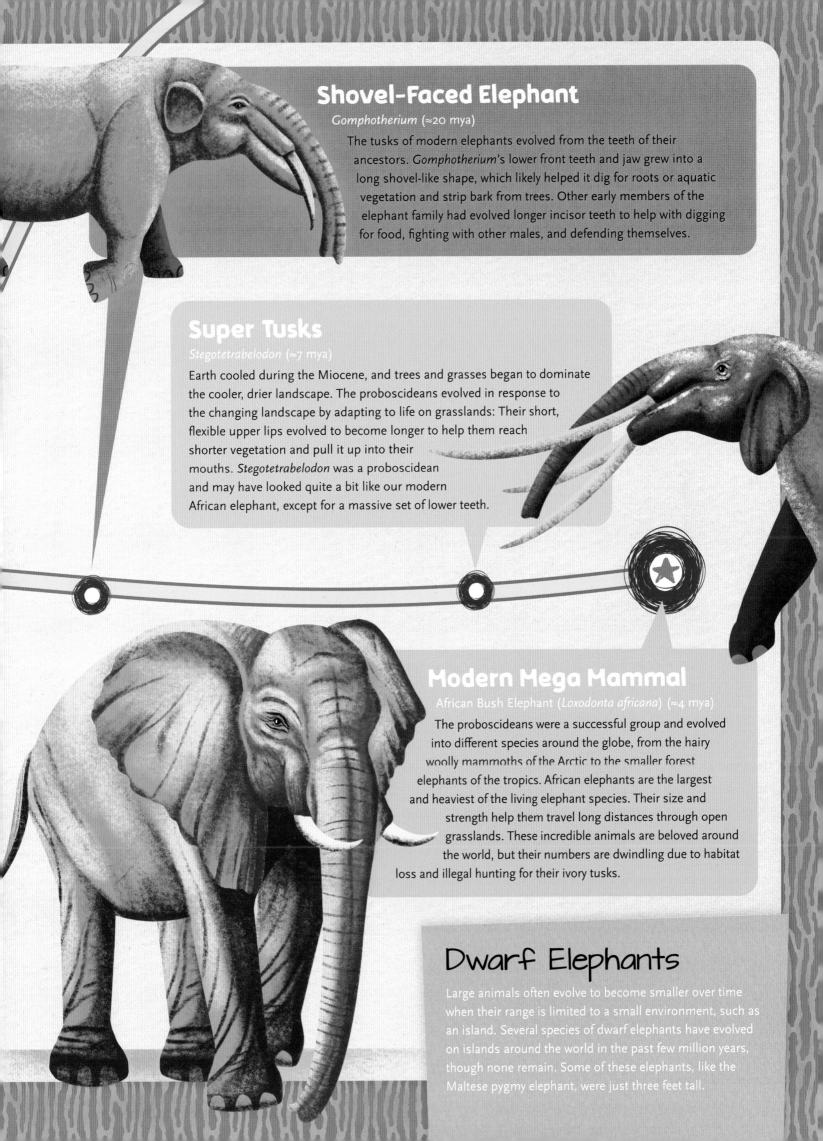

Shovel-Faced Elephant

Gomphotherium (≈20 mya)

The tusks of modern elephants evolved from the teeth of their ancestors. *Gomphotherium*'s lower front teeth and jaw grew into a long shovel-like shape, which likely helped it dig for roots or aquatic vegetation and strip bark from trees. Other early members of the elephant family had evolved longer incisor teeth to help with digging for food, fighting with other males, and defending themselves.

Super Tusks

Stegotetrabelodon (≈7 mya)

Earth cooled during the Miocene, and trees and grasses began to dominate the cooler, drier landscape. The proboscideans evolved in response to the changing landscape by adapting to life on grasslands: Their short, flexible upper lips evolved to become longer to help them reach shorter vegetation and pull it up into their mouths. *Stegotetrabelodon* was a proboscidean and may have looked quite a bit like our modern African elephant, except for a massive set of lower teeth.

Modern Mega Mammal

African Bush Elephant (*Loxodonta africana*) (≈4 mya)

The proboscideans were a successful group and evolved into different species around the globe, from the hairy woolly mammoths of the Arctic to the smaller forest elephants of the tropics. African elephants are the largest and heaviest of the living elephant species. Their size and strength help them travel long distances through open grasslands. These incredible animals are beloved around the world, but their numbers are dwindling due to habitat loss and illegal hunting for their ivory tusks.

Dwarf Elephants

Large animals often evolve to become smaller over time when their range is limited to a small environment, such as an island. Several species of dwarf elephants have evolved on islands around the world in the past few million years, though none remain. Some of these elephants, like the Maltese pygmy elephant, were just three feet tall.

MEXICAN FREE-TAILED BAT

Bats began as tree-climbing, insect-eating mammals and were so successful that they evolved to become more than 1,400 different species across the globe. They evolved a number of traits to help them in the air, including thin wings of skin between their fingers to help them fly and a special way to "see" insect prey flying in the dark.

Bats range from the massive flying foxes in the Southern Hemisphere, which can grow a wingspan of more than five feet, to what might be the smallest mammal in the world: the inch-long bumblebee bat of Southeast Asia. The Mexican free-tailed bat is one of the most numerous bats in the world, with a range that includes both North and South America. Millions of individual free-tailed bats roost together in caves across their range, which provide shelter and keep them safe from predators.

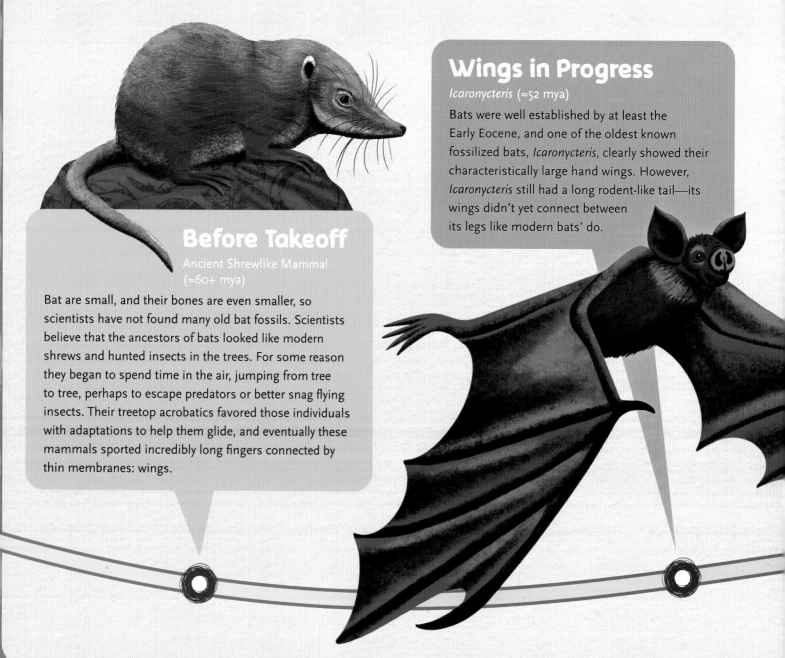

Wings in Progress
Icaronycteris (≈52 mya)

Bats were well established by at least the Early Eocene, and one of the oldest known fossilized bats, *Icaronycteris*, clearly showed their characteristically large hand wings. However, *Icaronycteris* still had a long rodent-like tail—its wings didn't yet connect between its legs like modern bats' do.

Before Takeoff
Ancient Shrewlike Mammal (≈60+ mya)

Bat are small, and their bones are even smaller, so scientists have not found many old bat fossils. Scientists believe that the ancestors of bats looked like modern shrews and hunted insects in the trees. For some reason they began to spend time in the air, jumping from tree to tree, perhaps to escape predators or better snag flying insects. Their treetop acrobatics favored those individuals with adaptations to help them glide, and eventually these mammals sported incredibly long fingers connected by thin membranes: wings.

Flight Pattern

Wings have evolved several times throughout history but never in the same way. Insects were the first to fly, 350 million years ago, and their wings likely evolved from one of their body segments. Pterosaurs were the first vertebrates to fly, on wings of skin hung from a single long finger. Feathers originally used for dinosaur decoration and warmth eventually helped birds take to the skies. And bat wings evolved from skin between each of their fingers.

Night Hunter

Wallia (≈42 mya)

Wallia is the oldest known of the free-tailed bats, which hunt insects at night using echolocation. It possibly evolved from sounds used to communicate with one another; bats learned to understand the physical world around them by listening to how noises bounced off objects and returned to their ears. The ability to hunt at night was a huge benefit to bats, which now had access to lots of food at a time of day when there were fewer predators.

Cave Crowds

Mexican Free-Tailed Bat
(*Tadarida brasiliensis*) (≈6.5 mya)

Bats use their strong claws to roost, or sleep, in places where predators can't find them, like under bridges and in tree cavities, rock crevices, and caves. Caves provide both reliable weather and protection from predators. The Mexican free-tailed bat is famous for inhabiting certain caves in huge numbers; the Bracken Cave near San Antonio, Texas, is home to an estimated 15 million bats on a given night.

Swarming Strategy

Bats are vulnerable to hawks when they leave their caves at dusk, but leaving all at once in a huge swarm can help disorient and overwhelm predators. It can take up to three hours for the multiple millions of bats to leave Bracken Cave each night.

MOOSE

The mighty moose is the largest living member of the deer family. Each year male moose grow a special set of large bones on their heads called antlers. While antlers may be used to defend a moose from a predator like a wolf, their primary purpose is to impress females. Female moose prefer males with larger antlers, as they may signify a stronger, healthier potential mate. The moose and its giant antlers live in the northern forests of North America, Europe, and Asia, growing to nearly seven feet tall and weighing up to a whopping 1,500 pounds. Their ancestors were smaller, however, and evolved a number of special traits to help them digest a plant-based diet and stay one step ahead of hungry predators.

Tiptoe Runner

Diacodexis (≈55 mya)

The earliest known artiodactyl was *Diacodexis*, a rabbit-sized herbivore. *Diacodexis* needed to be fast to evade predators, and its ancestors had built up their speed by evolving to run on their toes, which was faster than running flat-footed. They also evolved long, strong, and flexible limbs and sported tough hooves. Made out of a substance called keratin, hooves helped *Diacodexis* run on hard surfaces and could also be used to kick any predator that got too close.

A New Chew

Leptomeryx (≈34 mya)

The small deerlike *Leptomeryx* was part of a group of artiodactyls called the ruminants, which evolved special stomachs that allowed them to return partially digested food to their mouths for additional chewing. Rechewing its food maximized the nutrition from every mouthful and also let *Leptomeryx* keep its head up while chewing—better to keep an eye out for predators—instead of having to put its head down to graze.

Vampire Deer

Some of the strangest members of the deer family are the water deer (*Hydropotes inermis*), found in Asia. Instead of antlers, male water deer grow long fangs! These impressive teeth serve the same purpose as antlers: to fend off rival males and impress females.

To pigs and hippos, and to the blue whale, page 74

Antlers Away!

The rapid growth of deer antlers each year makes them the fastest growing type of bone known to science. The largest antlers in history were 12 feet wide and belonged to a giant Ice Age elk called Megaloceros giganteus.

To deer, elk, caribou, and others

Horn Section

Dicrocerus (≈10 mya)

The two-foot-tall *Dicrocerus* was one of the first known members of the deer family to have antlers. Scientists believe that *Dicrocerus* used its antlers to fight over females. Most modern deer grow antlers for the breeding season and then drop, or "shed," them when breeding season is over.

Huge Horns

Cervalces scotti (≈2 mya)

Some of the deer family made homes in wetland bogs, eating aquatic plants like lilies and milfoils. They grew large, and their size and thick fur helped them survive cold winters. *Cervalces scotti* was one of the largest deer to ever exist and likely looked and acted much like modern moose, except for larger and more irregular antlers.

Forest Giant

Moose (*Alces alces*) (≈2 mya)

Cervalces scotti went extinct about 11,500 years ago, perhaps due to overhunting from newly arrived humans, a change in climate, or disease. However, its contemporary *Alces alces* somehow survived. The moose is the largest member of the deer family alive today, standing more than six feet tall and weighing up to 1,500 pounds. Much like their cousin *Cervalces scotti*, moose prefer aquatic plants and have evolved special nostrils that can be sealed shut when they have their heads underwater.

To the giraffe, page 72

GIRAFFE

Giraffes are bewildering creatures: huge, hoofed mammals with heads perched upon supersized necks. Their massive size, spotted yellow patterning, and nearly two-foot-long tongues combine to make giraffes some of the most recognizable animals on the entire planet.

Giraffes are members of the family Giraffidae, a close relative of Cervidae (moose, deer) and Bovidae (sheep, goats, cows, buffalo). Believe it or not, most extinct Giraffidae species had short necks. The only other living member of Giraffidae besides giraffes, the okapi of central African forests, still has one. But giraffes evolved in a different direction, and competition for food and for mates stretched their necks to incredible lengths.

← From Leptomeryx, page 70

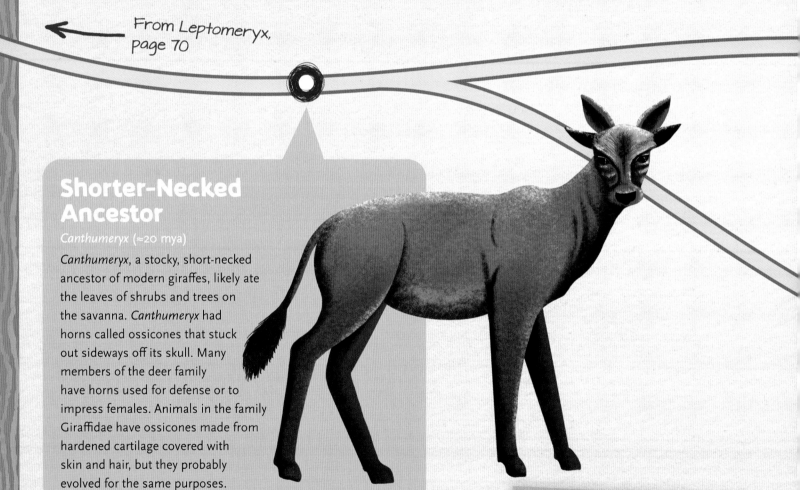

Shorter-Necked Ancestor

Canthumeryx (≈20 mya)

Canthumeryx, a stocky, short-necked ancestor of modern giraffes, likely ate the leaves of shrubs and trees on the savanna. *Canthumeryx* had horns called ossicones that stuck out sideways off its skull. Many members of the deer family have horns used for defense or to impress females. Animals in the family Giraffidae have ossicones made from hardened cartilage covered with skin and hair, but they probably evolved for the same purposes.

Tricky Tongue

Giraffes evolved long necks to help them reach the highest leaves, and they evolved a long, strong tongue and flexible upper lip that work together to grasp branches and deftly remove the leaves.

Giant Giraffe

Modern giraffes are the largest known giraffids, but a close second is *Sivatherium*. Living in Africa about seven million years ago, *Sivatherium* wasn't as tall as modern giraffes and didn't have a long neck, but it was thicker and had large antlerlike ossicones.

Stretching Out
Samotherium (≈15 mya)

The ancestors of modern giraffes began to sport longer and longer necks. *Samotherium*, from the Miocene, had long swept-back ossicones and a neck somewhere in length between that of the modern okapi and modern giraffe. Darwin suggested that the evolutionary explanation for these growing necks was that competition for leaves among antelope and other short species meant that those with longer necks could reach more food. While Darwin's theory still holds up, scientists believe that sexual selection may also have played a role in the growth of giraffe necks. Male giraffes battle over females by swinging their horned heads at each other, and longer necks might be better for fighting.

A View from the Top
Giraffe (*Giraffa camelopardalis*) (≈1 mya)

Full-grown male giraffes stand 18 feet tall—with about 8 feet of that made up of their long necks. They've had to evolve unusual bodies to carry such massive necks, including massive hearts to keep blood pumping up to their heads. Several subspecies of giraffes are spread throughout Africa, each distinguished by different blotchy patterns on their sides. Though it seems that nothing could hide these giant creatures, their spotted coloration is actually a form of camouflage, helping them blend in with their yellow-and-brown savanna landscapes.

To okapis →

BLUE WHALE

Believe it or not, the ancestors of whales were roughly the size and shape of rabbits. For millions of years after the dinosaurs went extinct, there were few large animals in the oceans besides sharks. Then a group of mammals waded back into water and began wading farther and farther out to evade predators and find food. There they diversified into different shapes and sizes, from relatively small fish-eating dolphins and porpoises to massive whales, including the largest animal that has ever lived on Earth: the blue whale.

The 100-foot-long blue whale can be found in oceans around the world. Despite its size, it feeds on tiny shrimplike creatures called krill. Swallowed in gigantic mouthfuls, the blue whale eats around 2,500 pounds of krill per day.

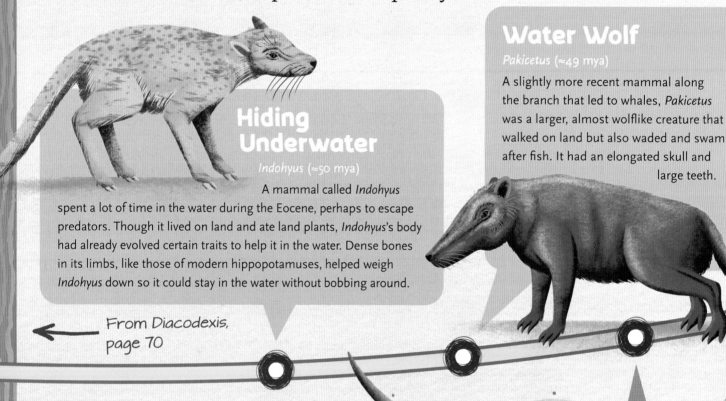

Water Wolf
Pakicetus (≈49 mya)

A slightly more recent mammal along the branch that led to whales, *Pakicetus* was a larger, almost wolflike creature that walked on land but also waded and swam after fish. It had an elongated skull and large teeth.

Hiding Underwater
Indohyus (≈50 mya)

A mammal called *Indohyus* spent a lot of time in the water during the Eocene, perhaps to escape predators. Though it lived on land and ate land plants, *Indohyus*'s body had already evolved certain traits to help it in the water. Dense bones in its limbs, like those of modern hippopotamuses, helped weigh *Indohyus* down so it could stay in the water without bobbing around.

From Diacodexis, page 70

Whaling Woes

Humans have hunted whales for thousands of years for their meat and oil, but highly organized and efficient hunting in the 18th and 19th centuries severely reduced whale populations. Hunting prohibitions and restrictions have helped stabilize many whale populations, but severe threats remain from climate change, being hit by boats, getting tangled up in ropes and nets from abandoned fishing gear, and human overfishing of whales' food sources. The blue whale is considered an endangered species, with somewhere between just 5,000 and 15,000 remaining in the world's oceans today.

Croco-Mammal
Ambulocetus (≈47 mya)

The seal-sized *Ambulocetus* was a step closer to living only in the water. It glided smoothly through the water like an otter and used its long jaws to clamp down on fish. It was thought to have been an ambush predator, like the crocodile, lying in wait and then lunging after prey.

Deep Breath

Unlike fish, which can pull oxygen out of the water through gills, whales and other marine mammals need to breathe air at the surface. A whale that feeds deep underwater must take a breath at the surface and hold it for its entire dive, which can last more than two hours. The Cuvier's beaked whale is the current record holder, staying underwater for more than two hours as it dived at depths near 10,000 feet in pursuit of squid.

Feet to Flippers

Protocetus (≈45 mya)

"*Protocetus*" means "first whale," and it spent all its time in the water. In *Protocetus*, the front limbs of its walking ancestors had evolved webbing between the fingers and toes to help it swim, and the back limbs were on their way to being lost entirely. Its tail, which had been long like a dog's in its ancestors, had evolved to become flat like a whale's, helping propel the animal underwater.

Breathing Easy

Basilosaurus (≈41 mya)

Now firmly at home underwater, whales began to grow large—and hungry. The 50-foot-long *Basilosaurus* may have been the apex predator of its time and hunted for sharks and smaller whales. As whales evolved, their nostrils moved from the fronts of their faces up to the tops of their heads, eventually becoming blowholes. Top-mounted breathing is more convenient for swimming whales because they can keep their heads and eyes underwater while they breathe.

To killer whales, sperm whales, dolphins, and porpoises

To right whales, humpback whales, gray whales, and others

A New Diet

Llanocetus (≈37 mya)

Llanocetus was one of the oldest known of a group of whales that stopped hunting large prey and instead began to gulp down massive schools of tiny shrimplike krill. Though *Llanocetus* had teeth and is thought to have fed by sucking invertebrates and small fish into its mouth, scientists studying its fossilized teeth have spotted the origins of the filters used by the modern blue whale.

Marine Mammoth

Blue Whale
(*Balaenoptera musculus*) (≈10 mya)

As large as it is, the giant blue whale dines on tiny krill. To get enough to eat, these whales take in big mouthfuls of water and then filter out the food; the water flows through long bristles of keratin called baleen, and the krill are left behind. A blue whale takes in a swimming pool's worth of water with each gulp and filters out about four tons of krill per day as food.

HORSE

The evolution of horses into one of our more important allies spanned millions of years.

Though horses are similar in many ways to deer, antelope, and other hoofed mammals in the artiodactyl group, they are actually part of a separate group called perissodactyls. Both groups of mammals are plant eaters that evolved great speed to stay ahead of predators, but early perissodactyl mammals evolved a different arrangement of toes. Today, perissodactyls are represented by just a few living families: rhinoceroses, tapirs, and equines, which includes horses and zebras.

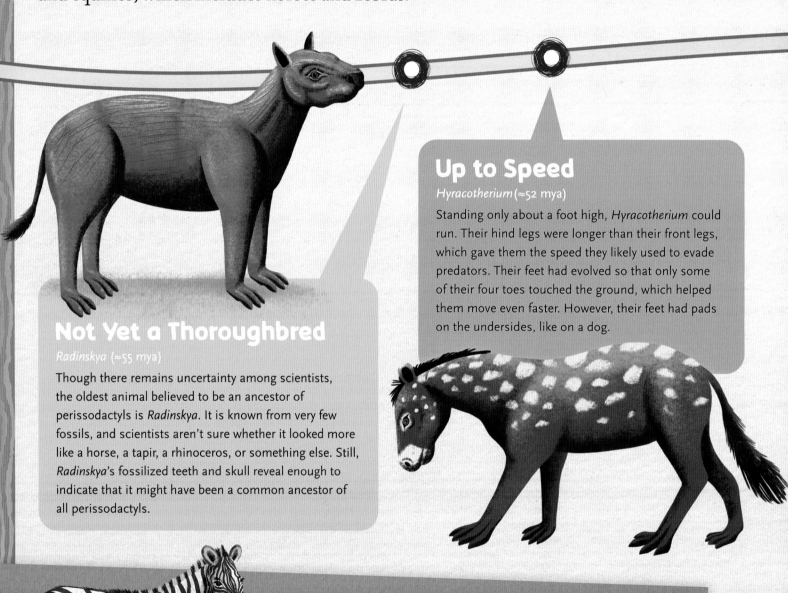

Not Yet a Thoroughbred

Radinskya (≈55 mya)

Though there remains uncertainty among scientists, the oldest animal believed to be an ancestor of perissodactyls is *Radinskya*. It is known from very few fossils, and scientists aren't sure whether it looked more like a horse, a tapir, a rhinoceros, or something else. Still, *Radinskya*'s fossilized teeth and skull reveal enough to indicate that it might have been a common ancestor of all perissodactyls.

Up to Speed

Hyracotherium (≈52 mya)

Standing only about a foot high, *Hyracotherium* could run. Their hind legs were longer than their front legs, which gave them the speed they likely used to evade predators. Their feet had evolved so that only some of their four toes touched the ground, which helped them move even faster. However, their feet had pads on the undersides, like on a dog.

Earning Their Stripes

Zebras are among the few close relatives of horses still around today. Scientists have long debated the purpose of the zebra's bold black-and-white stripes and believe now that the pattern evolved to deter biting flies from landing.

Even Faster

Mesohippus (≈40 mya)

During the Eocene, small horses flourished, including *Mesohippus*. About two feet tall, *Mesohippus* had three toes on each leg, with the middle toe extending farther than the ones on either side. Much of these creatures' evolution during this time was in response to environmental changes. Forests were giving way to open grasslands, meaning that speed was even more important. *Mesohippus* was also eating more grass now than fruits, and the teeth of early horses evolved to grind down tougher plants.

To zebras, Przewalski's horses, and others →

A Horse, of Course

Horse (*Equus caballus*) (≈1 mya)

Modern horses appeared about one million years ago, during the Pleistocene epoch. Humans domesticated horses about 6,000 years ago, likely riding the speedy creatures to hunt down other prey and using them for agricultural work. Today, millions of domestic horses in the world provide companionship, labor, and recreation.

Mostly Modern

Dinohippus (≈10 mya)

A sure-footed speedster of the grassy Pliocene plains, *Dinohippus* looked very much like a modern horse. The long central toe had become a single, strong hoof, helping *Dinohippus* run fast across hard-packed grasslands. Its teeth were longer and bumpier than those of previous horses, better to withstand the constant grinding required when eating mostly grass.

Horsing Around

As with many domesticated animals and plants, humans have bred horses into all sorts of different shapes and sizes. Humans breed select horses with desirable traits—like strength or speed or size—and then breed them, hoping their offspring will also inherit those traits. Humans have guided the evolution of horses into large, muscular workhorses like the Clydesdale; lean, fast racehorses; small, docile ponies; and other forms.

NORTH AMERICAN PORCUPINE

The need to stay safe from predators is one of the major drivers of evolution. **Some animals, like horses and gazelles, have run away from danger and evolved to become fast and agile.** Some, like the snowshoe hare, have stayed safe by hiding from predators and evolved elaborate camouflage. Others, such as prairie dogs, hide underground. Porcupines defend themselves with spiky armor. These docile animals evolved a thick coat of sharp spines to give any creature that tries to mess with them a painful bite.

Porcupines are part of a large family of mammals called rodents. Ranging from the two-inch-long African pygmy mouse to the four-foot-long capybara, rodents come in all shapes and sizes, but they all have one thing in common: sharp front teeth that grow nonstop. Rodents use these teeth to gnaw on food, chew through wood, dig underground, and defend themselves.

To rabbits, rats, mice, beavers, gophers, squirrels, and others

Signature Smile

Tribosphenomys (≈56 mya)

Rodents can be traced in the fossil record back to more than 50 million years ago, though molecular research indicates that they're likely millions of years older. One of the oldest rodents we know of was *Tribosphenomys*, which lived in what is now Asia. Little is known about what *Tribosphenomys* looked like, but it was probably about the same size as a modern rat, and its fossilized jaws clearly show the beginnings of rodents' trademark front teeth.

Don't Shoot!

Some people used to believe that porcupines could shoot their quills at attackers, but that's not true. However, quills detach easily from a porcupine's body once they've stuck into a predator in order to help the porcupine get away.

Air Rodent

Rodents are the most diverse of all mammals, with more than 1,500 different species alive today. They can burrow, swim, and even fly. The flying squirrel has evolved long folds of skin between its front and back legs that act as a sort of parachute. Flying squirrels climb high in trees and then leap into the air and spread their limbs, gliding on their skin flap "wings" for up to 500 feet, if necessary.

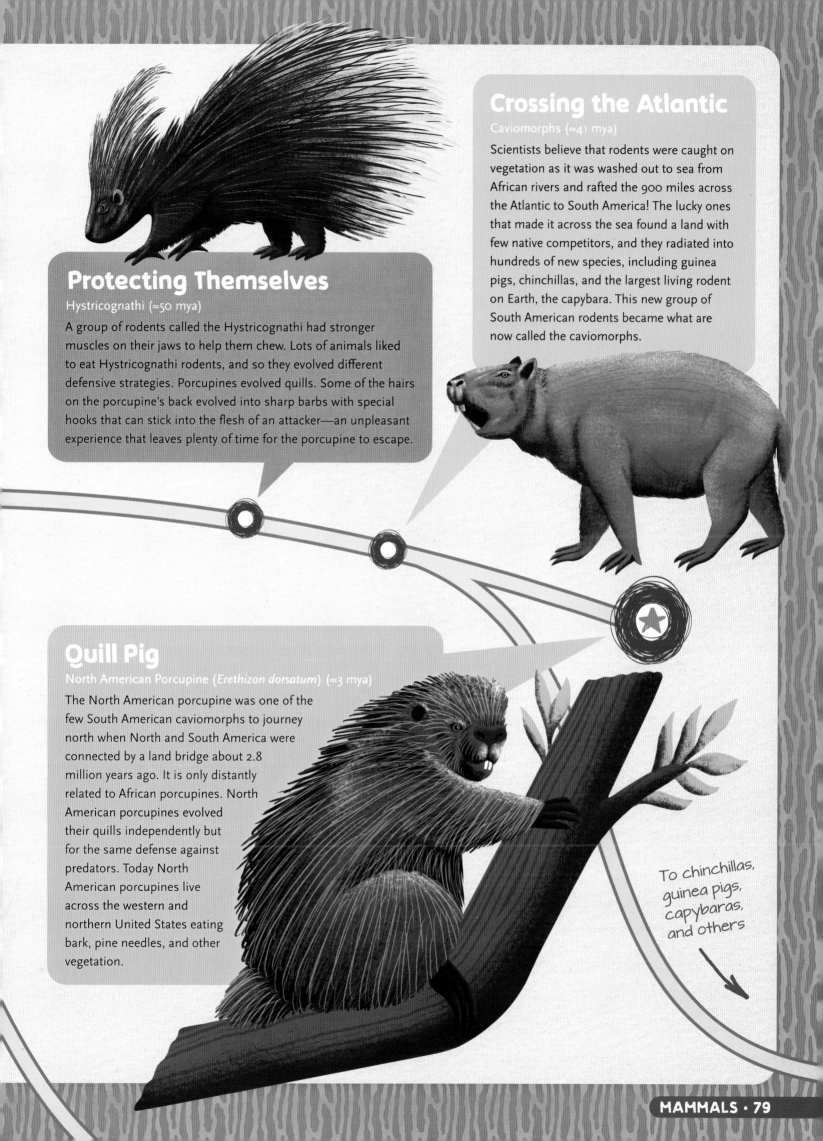

Protecting Themselves
Hystricognathi (≈50 mya)

A group of rodents called the Hystricognathi had stronger muscles on their jaws to help them chew. Lots of animals liked to eat Hystricognathi rodents, and so they evolved different defensive strategies. Porcupines evolved quills. Some of the hairs on the porcupine's back evolved into sharp barbs with special hooks that can stick into the flesh of an attacker—an unpleasant experience that leaves plenty of time for the porcupine to escape.

Crossing the Atlantic
Caviomorphs (≈41 mya)

Scientists believe that rodents were caught on vegetation as it was washed out to sea from African rivers and rafted the 900 miles across the Atlantic to South America! The lucky ones that made it across the sea found a land with few native competitors, and they radiated into hundreds of new species, including guinea pigs, chinchillas, and the largest living rodent on Earth, the capybara. This new group of South American rodents became what are now called the caviomorphs.

Quill Pig
North American Porcupine (*Erethizon dorsatum*) (≈3 mya)

The North American porcupine was one of the few South American caviomorphs to journey north when North and South America were connected by a land bridge about 2.8 million years ago. It is only distantly related to African porcupines. North American porcupines evolved their quills independently but for the same defense against predators. Today North American porcupines live across the western and northern United States eating bark, pine needles, and other vegetation.

To chinchillas, guinea pigs, capybaras, and others

CAT

Cats and dogs are some of our best friends, but they both evolved from fierce wild animals. They are both members of a family of meat-eating mammals called carnivorans. The order Carnivora is home to the most fearsome predators on Earth, like lions and polar bears, as well as some of our snuggliest cats and dogs.

The animals that evolved into modern cats and dogs split from a common ancestor onto different branches of the Tree of Life some 60 million years ago. Each branch evolved their own methods for hunting prey. The cat branch, called the felids, evolved to become ambush hunters. Cats have extremely good eyesight and smell, which help them spot prey before it spots them. Camouflage coloration aids their secrecy. Depending on the environment, cats will either silently stalk prey until they're close enough to strike, or they'll wait for prey to come close and then lunge forward, scratching with sharp claws and clamping down with sharp teeth.

Early Hunter
Miacids (≈60 mya)
Among the ancestors of the carnivorans was a group of weasel-sized predators called the miacids, which likely hunted both in the trees and on the ground. They had sharp claws and knifelike teeth to kill prey, as well as acute senses to help them hunt.

Branching Out
Pseudaelurus (≈20 mya)
Stalking animals in the treetops requires ultimate balance and stealth. *Pseudaelurus* had a long tail, short legs, and a long body, all helping it stay balanced in the canopy. This early cat evolved in what is now Europe but spread around the globe, and several different cat lines are believed to have evolved from *Pseudaelurus* species.

To the dog and to bears →

Fast Cat
Cheetahs are large cats that hunt on the open savanna. Stalking is more difficult when there's little to hide behind, so the cheetah has evolved to be as fast as possible, with a thin body, strong legs, and a long tail to help it stay balanced while chasing prey. These adaptations have helped the cheetah become the world's fastest land animal, sprinting at speeds up to 60 miles per hour.

The Element of Surprise
African Wildcat (*Felis lybica*) (≈2 mya)
The African wildcat is one species of small feline that uses stealth and speed to pounce on mice, rats, birds, and insects. It's believed that African wildcats began their relationship with humans by hunting rodents around the fields of early farmers in the Middle East.

Friendly Feline
Cat (*Felis catus*) (≈9,500 years ago)
Cats eventually became domesticated, and they were soon chasing mice inside homes. Humans have selectively bred cats into dozens of different types—short-haired, long-haired, all different colors—and have made cats one of the most common pets in the world.

DOG

Dogs, from the canid branch of the Tree of Life, were generally more social than cats, living and hunting in packs. They evolved to be pursuit hunters, meaning they form groups to tirelessly chase after prey until it reaches the point of exhaustion. They evolved endurance and social bonds to help them bring down prey as a team.

Tree Dog

Hesperocyon (≈40 mya)

The oldest fossil in the Canidae line is *Hesperocyon*, which may have looked something like a modern-day mongoose or fox. Like the earliest cats, it may have hunted mostly in trees, but it was likely already showing adaptations for life on the ground, including longer limbs and more-forward-facing toes that were better for running.

Working Together

Gray Wolf (*Canis Lupus*)
(≈200,000 years ago)

Canids reached their predatory apex with the wolves. The secret to the wolf's success is cooperative hunting. Chasing a deer or horse over open ground is difficult and exhausting, but somewhere along the line, wolves learned to hunt in packs. Different members of the pack can take turns sprinting after a single animal, or they can attack from different angles and cut off escape.

To lions, cheetahs, mountain lions, and others

Best Friend's Beginnings

Dog (*Canis familiaris*) (≈15,000 years ago)

The exact timing of the domestication of dogs is unclear, but it occurred at least 15,000 years ago. It's presumed that wolves were attracted to the carcasses of large animals killed by early humans. Over time, social wolves grew closer and closer to humans, and they eventually became domesticated. Humans have since steered the evolution of those earliest dogs into hundreds of different dog breeds.

Cold Dog

One canid, the arctic fox, has evolved special traits to permit it to live in some of the coldest areas on Earth. It has very thick fur covering its body—including its feet—to keep it warm, and short ears and limbs as well as a short snout to minimize heat loss. To help it blend into its surroundings, the arctic fox grows a snow-white coat in the winter and a brownish coat in the summer.

MANTLED HOWLER MONKEY

Primates is the order of mammals that includes monkeys, apes, and humans. Our family origins began in the Paleocene epoch more than 50 million years ago. The earliest primates lived in the trees and evolved certain traits to help them adapt to a life aboveground, including good vision to help them find ripe fruit, dexterous hands to help them grasp thin branches, and large brains. These traits and others set some primates on a course to eventually leave the trees, but many modern primates remain among the branches.

Howler monkeys live in the jungles of Central and South America. They are most famous for their loud calls, or "howls," which they use to communicate. Howler monkeys are considered among the loudest animals on land, as their howls can be heard for miles across the forest!

Transoceanic Primate

Perupithecus (≈36 mya)

Perupithecus lived in trees and may have looked and acted like earlier primates, but there was a major difference: It lived on the island continent of South America. Primates made the same incredible journey across the Atlantic as the rodents, hitching a ride on floating vegetation (see page 79). Once the primates made landfall, they found themselves without competition from other animals, and they quickly radiated into many new forms, including the ancestors of more than 70 species of monkeys living in South America today.

Improved Eyesight

Earliest Primates (≈74 mya)

Though there remains much to learn about the earliest ancestors of the primates, scientists believe that the group originated in what is now Asia during the Eocene epoch. One of the most important adaptations found in some of the earliest primates was forward-facing eyes, which provide better depth perception, and allowed early primates like *Archicebus* to move more confidently through the trees in search of insects.

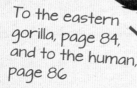

To the eastern gorilla, page 84, and to the human, page 86

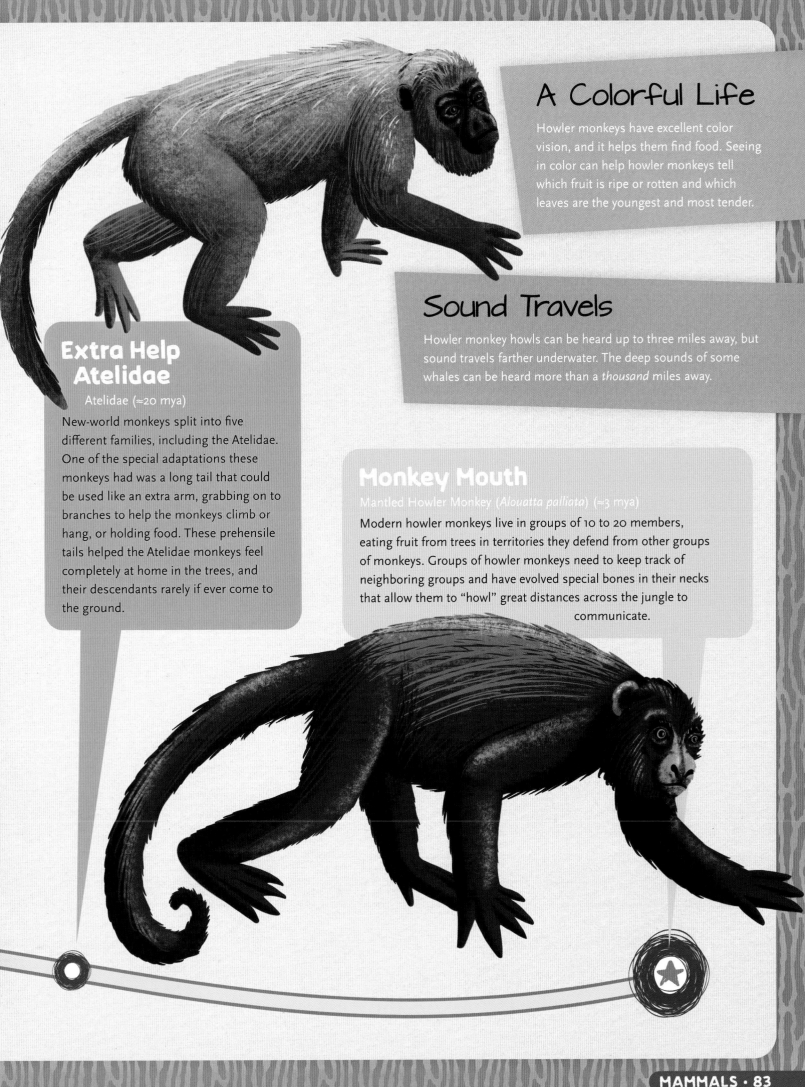

A Colorful Life

Howler monkeys have excellent color vision, and it helps them find food. Seeing in color can help howler monkeys tell which fruit is ripe or rotten and which leaves are the youngest and most tender.

Sound Travels

Howler monkey howls can be heard up to three miles away, but sound travels farther underwater. The deep sounds of some whales can be heard more than a *thousand* miles away.

Extra Help
Atelidae

Atelidae (≈20 mya)

New-world monkeys split into five different families, including the Atelidae. One of the special adaptations these monkeys had was a long tail that could be used like an extra arm, grabbing on to branches to help the monkeys climb or hang, or holding food. These prehensile tails helped the Atelidae monkeys feel completely at home in the trees, and their descendants rarely if ever come to the ground.

Monkey Mouth

Mantled Howler Monkey (*Alouatta palliata*) (≈3 mya)

Modern howler monkeys live in groups of 10 to 20 members, eating fruit from trees in territories they defend from other groups of monkeys. Groups of howler monkeys need to keep track of neighboring groups and have evolved special bones in their necks that allow them to "howl" great distances across the jungle to communicate.

EASTERN GORILLA

Primates originally evolved in Asia and Africa, and they continued to evolve there into diverse groups. Some became the old-world monkeys, which include baboons and macaques. Others became hominids, also known as great apes. The largest great ape, and the largest living primate of all, is the gorilla. Living only in the forests of central Africa, the planet's two gorilla species, eastern and western, are both critically endangered.

Swing Set

Rukwapithecus (≈25 mya)

Fossils of *Rukwapithecus* may represent the oldest known hominoid after the split between apes and old-world monkeys. Still mainly tree dwelling in the Miocene epoch, apes in the next few million years after *Rukwapithecus* eventually evolved special shoulder joints to help them move through the branches. Instead of walking on all fours and jumping from limb to limb like other monkeys, apes could hang from their hands and swing through the treetops.

From the earliest primates, page 82

Social Life

Gorillas, like all apes, are very social. They live in groups called troops, each led by a dominant older male gorilla called a silverback. When male gorillas reach about 12 years old, they develop gray hair on their backs. The presence of a silver back indicates that a male gorilla is ready to lead a group.

To gibbons

To orangutans

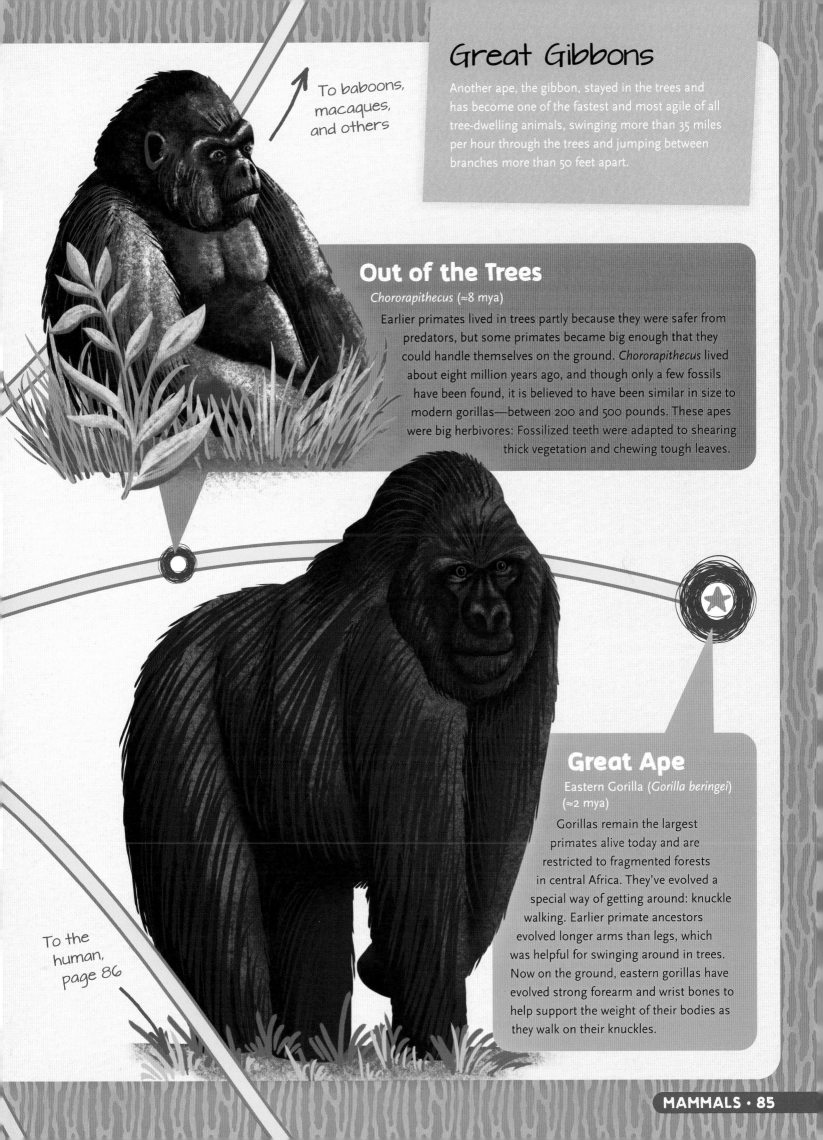

Great Gibbons

Another ape, the gibbon, stayed in the trees and has become one of the fastest and most agile of all tree-dwelling animals, swinging more than 35 miles per hour through the trees and jumping between branches more than 50 feet apart.

To baboons, macaques, and others

Out of the Trees

Chororapithecus (≈8 mya)

Earlier primates lived in trees partly because they were safer from predators, but some primates became big enough that they could handle themselves on the ground. *Chororapithecus* lived about eight million years ago, and though only a few fossils have been found, it is believed to have been similar in size to modern gorillas—between 200 and 500 pounds. These apes were big herbivores: Fossilized teeth were adapted to shearing thick vegetation and chewing tough leaves.

Great Ape

Eastern Gorilla (*Gorilla beringei*) (≈2 mya)

Gorillas remain the largest primates alive today and are restricted to fragmented forests in central Africa. They've evolved a special way of getting around: knuckle walking. Earlier primate ancestors evolved longer arms than legs, which was helpful for swinging around in trees. Now on the ground, eastern gorillas have evolved strong forearm and wrist bones to help support the weight of their bodies as they walk on their knuckles.

To the human, page 86

HUMAN

In many ways, humans, the species *Homo sapiens*, are just another species of life on Earth. We are the products of the same evolutionary forces that shape all life. Our ancestors had to figure out ways to stay safe. We had to stay fed and feed our growing babies. We had to survive.

The ancestors of humans evolved a number of critical adaptations. We evolved to walk on two legs, freeing up our hands to hold tools and food and allowing us to move quickly over open ground. Most important, our ancestors evolved large, complex brains. Our brains gave us the ability to solve problems that no other creatures could—how to build fire, make clothing, domesticate animals and plants—giving us massive advantages for survival.

Scientists aren't completely sure how the human branch of the Tree of Life grew, but they're making new discoveries all the time. What's clear is that we split away from our primate relatives sometime in the past few million years and then, relatively quickly, evolved into the incredible species we are today.

Standing Up for Ourselves

Sahelanthropus tchadensis (≈7 mya)

The skull of this ape, found in the country of Chad, may be a common ancestor of both humans and chimpanzees, or it may have evolved along the human line somewhere after the split. *Sahelanthropus* had a mix of apelike features, including a small brain and a large brow, and human features, like small canine teeth and a flatter face than earlier apes. It also stood upright. The ability to walk upright was, quite literally, a huge step forward.

Walking On

Australopithecus (≈4 mya)

There are several known species of *Australopithecus*, including the famous remains of an *Australopithecus afarensis* known as Lucy. These animals were smaller and thinner than modern humans—the species varied between three and five feet, and males are generally thought to have been larger than females. While it's believed that the australopithecines were bipedal, meaning they walked on two feet, their skeletons also suggest that they may have spent significant time climbing trees.

To chimpanzees

Using Tools

Homo habilis (≈2.5 mya)

Bipedalism freed up the hands of early humans and *Homo habilis* used them to make tools. Paleontologists have found evidence of tool use as far back as *Australopithecus*, and *Homo habilis* sites reveal the use of stone tools, including hammers and slicers, that were likely used to cut meat and skin from dead animals.

To Neanderthals

Rapid Advancement

Homo erectus (≈1.9 mya)

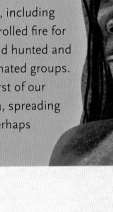

Homo erectus experienced incredible advancements over its existence, which is thought to have lasted until about 110,000 years ago. *Homo erectus* had proportions more like modern humans, adapted for walking and running and not for a life in the trees. Aided by an energy-rich diet of meat, *Homo erectus* possessed a larger brain than that of earlier hominins, and it made advancements in stone-tool technology, including making hand axes; controlled fire for cooking and warmth; and hunted and gathered food in coordinated groups. *Homo erectus* was the first of our ancestors to leave Africa, spreading out through Asia and perhaps into Europe.

Direct Ancestor?

Homo heidelbergensis (≈700,000 years ago)

Many scientists believe that *Homo heidelbergensis* may have been a direct ancestor of modern humans. These archaic humans lived in colder climates than other species and developed smaller bodies to help conserve heat. *Homo heidelbergensis*'s brains were nearly the size of modern humans', and the species is credited with several important milestones, including carving wooden spears to hunt large game and building the first known shelters, out of wood and stone.

You Are Here

Homo sapiens (≈300,000 years ago)

Every human being in the world is a member of *Homo sapiens*. Our species first appeared in Africa about 300,000 years ago, and as we grew, we encountered other living hominin species, including the Neanderthals, with whom we both outcompeted and interbred. We've spread around the globe, built cities, and even flown into space!

WHERE DOES EVOLUTION TAKE US FROM HERE?

Evolution has shaped all life on Earth over billions of years, and while we have no idea what the future holds, we do know that evolution will continue.

There has never been a species like humans on Earth, and we have advanced to a point where evolution doesn't affect us in quite the same way as it has other creatures throughout history. Our species has developed technologies that dampen the force of natural selection, which drives evolution. We can grow our own food and build structures to protect us from the weather, meaning we're not as susceptible to changes in climate. We have invented medicines to heal ourselves when we're sick. We've built weapons and fences to defend ourselves from any predators. The normal rules of evolution don't really apply to us anymore.

But we are still evolving. One way that humans are currently changing is that our species is mixing genes more quickly than ever before. Before the age of modern transportation, populations of humans in different parts of the world evolved to look different, in the same way isolated populations of many species evolve to look slightly different. But formerly isolated populations of humans now move and mix more often than ever before, meaning that our species is evolving to look more alike.

The future of human evolution is anyone's guess. Continued technological advancements may render natural selection totally obsolete, or, if things go wrong, they may bring about the end of our species altogether. Only time will tell.

However, evolution would continue in a world without humans. If the human race was lost in an extinction event—either a natural disaster like the asteroid that killed the dinosaurs or a human-caused disaster like war or climate change—any surviving species would eventually evolve to fill the void we left behind, as has happened in the wake of so many extinction events throughout Earth's history. Perhaps insects will rise up and become the planet's dominant group. Maybe rodents, maybe birds? There's no way of knowing, but we do know that life will go on changing and growing and evolving into new and amazing forms.

Glossary

ADAPTATION: A trait or characteristic that enhances an organism's ability to survive and reproduce in a specific environment. Adaptations arise through natural selection.

ANCESTOR: Any organism (either an individual or a species) that gives rise to additional organisms, its descendants.

COMMON ANCESTOR: An organism from which two or more different species have descended. Common ancestors represent points in evolutionary history where species diverged and began evolving along separate paths.

CONVERGENT EVOLUTION: The independent evolution of similar traits or adaptations in different species that do not share a recent common ancestor. Convergent evolution often occurs in response to similar environmental challenges or selective pressures.

DOMESTICATION: The process in which organisms are modified to become better suited to human use.

ENVIRONMENT: The natural space and ecosystem of a particular region.

EVOLUTION: The process of change in all forms of life over generations, involving the descent with modification of ancestral species to produce new species over time.

FOSSIL: The preserved remains or traces of ancient organisms found in rocks or other geological deposits. Fossils provide important evidence of past life forms and allow scientists to study the history of evolution.

GENERATION: A set of individuals that are born or hatched at about the same time, or the period corresponding to the time during which that set of individuals mature and produce the next generation themselves.

GENETIC VARIATION: The diversity of genetic material within a population or species. Genetic variation is the raw material upon which natural selection acts, allowing for the evolution of new traits.

HABITAT: The region associated with a particular species and favorable for its survival and way of life.

HERITABLE: In biology, the phenomenon in which information or characteristics can be passed down through generations.

INVERTEBRATES: A large group of organisms including all those species lacking bones: from single-celled creatures to mollusks and arthropods.

MUTATION: A random change in an organism's genetic material (DNA) that can give rise to new genetic variations. Mutations are a source of genetic diversity and can contribute to the evolution of species.

NATURAL SELECTION: The mechanism by which evolution occurs, driven by the differential survival and reproduction of individuals with favorable traits that are better suited to their environment.

PHYLOGENY: The evolutionary history and relationships among organisms. Phylogenetic trees or cladograms depict the branching patterns of species, indicating their shared ancestry and evolutionary connections.

POPULATION: Any group of living things that have a genetic connection, those members of a species inhabiting the same area, or a group of species that are being discussed together.

SPECIES: A fundamental unit of classification in biology. It refers to a group of organisms that share common characteristics and are capable of interbreeding to produce fertile offspring.

SPECIATION: The process by which new species arise. It occurs when populations of the same species become reproductively isolated from one another, leading to the accumulation of genetic differences over time.

VERTEBRATES: The group of organisms that possess bones: including fish, amphibians, reptiles, mammals, and their extinct relatives.

Suggestions for Further Reading

The Ascent of Birds: How Modern Science Is Revealing Their Story, John Reilly

Blue Planet series (2001), BBC

Bovids of the World: Antelopes, Gazelles, Cattle, Goats, Sheep, and Relatives (Princeton Field Guides, 104), José R. Castelló

Canids of the World: Wolves, Wild Dogs, Foxes, Jackals, Coyotes, and Their Relatives (Princeton Field Guides, 116), José R. Castelló

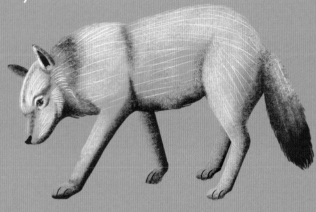

Darwin's Armada: Four Voyages and the Battle for the Theory of Evolution, Iain McCalman

Evolution in Minutes, Darren Naish

Evolution: Making Sense of Life, Douglas J. Emlen and Carl Zimmer

Evolution: The Human Story, 2nd ed., Alice Roberts

Evolution: What the Fossils Say and Why It Matters, Donald R. Prothero

Felids and Hyenas of the World: Wildcats, Panthers, Lynx, Pumas, Ocelots, Caracals, and Relatives (Princeton Field Guides), José R. Castelló

Life in Cold Blood series (2008), presented by David Attenborough

Life in the Undergrowth series (2005), presented by David Attenborough

The Life of Birds series (1998), presented by David Attenborough

The Life of Mammals series (2002), presented by David Attenborough

Peterson Field Guide to Freshwater Fishes, 2nd ed., Lawrence M. Page and Brooks M. Burr

The Princeton Field Guide to Prehistoric Mammals, Donald R. Prothero, illustrated by Mary Persis Williams

Reptiles and Amphibians, Herbert S. Zim and Hobart M. Smith

The Rise and Fall of the Dinosaurs, Steve Brusatte

The Sibley Guide to Birds, 2nd ed., David Allen Sibley

The Sibley Guide to Bird Life & Behavior, David Allen Sibley

The Story of Evolution in 25 Discoveries: The Evidence and the People Who Found It, Donald R. Prothero

Tetrapod Zoology: Book One, Darren Naish

Nick Lund

Nick Lund is a nature writer who mostly writes silly things about birds on Twitter when he should be working. He is the author of *The Ultimate Biography of Earth*, and his writing on birds and nature has appeared in *Audubon* magazine, *National Parks* magazine, Slate.com, the *Washington Post*, the *Maine Sportsman*, the *Portland Phoenix*, *Down East* magazine, and others. He is a graduate of the University of Maine School of Law and has worked in federal energy policy in Washington, DC, before returning to Maine with his wife and son to work for Maine Audubon.

Lucy Rose

Lucy Rose is a UK-based illustrator and surface pattern designer who graduated from Falmouth University with a BA in Illustration. She has always loved print processes and this is reflected in her work with organic textures and graphic compositions. Currently living in South Devon by the sea, Lucy takes inspiration from nature and the botanical elements that surround her.